A
WALK
IN THE
DARK

T0385247

A WALK IN THE DARK

JANE GODWIN

LOTHIAN

A Lothian Children's Book

Published in Australia and New Zealand in 2022
by Hachette Australia
(an imprint of Hachette Australia Pty Limited)
Gadigal Country, Level 17, 207 Kent Street, Sydney NSW 2000
www.hachettechildrens.com.au

Hachette Australia acknowledges and pays our respects to the past, present and future Traditional Owners and Custodians of Country throughout Australia and recognises the continuation of cultural, spiritual and educational practices of Aboriginal and Torres Strait Islander peoples. Our head office is located on the lands of the Gadigal people of the Eora Nation.

 A catalogue record for this book is available from the National Library of Australia

ISBN: 978 0 7344 2077 0 (paperback)

Cover illustration by David Dean
Cover design by Christabella Designs
Author photo: Lillie Thompson
Typeset in 11.2/16 pt Minion Pro by Bookhouse, Sydney
Printed and bound in Great Britain by Clays Ltd, Elcograf S.p.A.

MIX
Paper from
responsible sources
FSC® C001695

The paper this book is printed on is certified against the Forest Stewardship Council® Standards. McPherson's Printing Group holds FSC® chain of custody certification SA-COC-005379. FSC® promotes environmentally responsible, socially beneficial and economically viable management of the world's forests.

In memory of Ivan Southall

We grow accustomed to the Dark –
When Light is put away –
As when the Neighbor holds the Lamp
To witness her Goodbye –

A Moment – We uncertain step
For newness of the night –
Then – fit our Vision to the Dark –
And meet the Road – erect –

And so of larger – Darknesses –
Those Evenings of the Brain –
When not a Moon disclose a sign –
Or Star – come out – within –

The Bravest – grope a little –
And sometimes hit a Tree
Directly in the Forehead –
But as they learn to see –

Either the Darkness alters –
Or something in the sight
Adjusts itself to Midnight –
And Life steps almost straight.

Emily Dickinson

By this time a hundred years had passed,
the forest had grown and closed around the castle walls,
while everyone within them
slept.

Sleeping Beauty

One

Fred left without saying goodbye. Jess wasn't awake anyway. He'd had to get up early to catch the bus. Why did his mum make him go to this stupid school with its stupid hikes. He'd imagined it would be slack, a free school with no rules, but it wasn't. His dad had said Bellarine Grammar, and boarding, would sort Fred out, but it hadn't. Now it was his mum's turn for a social experiment. That's what he was. A social experiment.

He got on at Kennett River. The light was grey, it was just before dawn. Warm air inside formed condensation on the windows. The bus wound its way along the looping road that hugged the coast, following its shape. Fred couldn't look at his phone because looking down made him car-sick. Bus-sick. He listened to music instead. Violent Soho. Closed his eyes.

When he opened them again, the sun was rising over the ocean. The sea was silver and the sky was pink. Pink Madder Lake. Fred knew the colours because he'd had the Derwents. He forgot most of what he was taught at school, facts and history and science, but lately, the names of those coloured pencils had come back to him. He let himself watch the ocean, the pink horizon, for a moment. Fred supposed it looked beautiful, he supposed he could understand that this road, the Great Ocean Road, was world famous and tourists came here from everywhere, but it was also just the route to school.

His new school.

•

Ash got on at Skenes Creek. A chill washed in each time the bus door opened, hissing on its hinges. Kids in puffer jackets, beanies, eyes glistening in the cold of the morning.

'Hey, Fred.' Ash was smiling. He always was.

Fred felt hungry. He hadn't had breakfast.

'I wonder where they'll drop us.' Ash settled his backpack under the seat in front.

Fred took out an earbud. 'Have you done this before?'

Ash shook his head. 'Been camping heaps of times, but not on my own, not a dropping.'

Fred thought it sounded like bird poo. A dropping.

'So they really drive us somewhere and drop us off?' he asked.

Ash nodded, putting in his buds.

•

As the sky lightened, the bus turned from the coast and headed inland to rolling hills and dairy farms. It had been a wet March, and the hills were emerald green. Black-and-white cows stood in the foreground like a painting. Fred knew Emerald Green, too, from the Derwent pencil. There was a girl at this new school called Emerald, as well. When Fred was a kid he drew

2

all the time, but not anymore. Music, YouTube and PlayStation were what he did now. In the pack of seventy-two Derwents, there were twelve greens. Fred could picture Emerald Green and Bottle Green. And Olive. Was there a Sea Green? Often the sea was green, but sometimes it was blue, or grey, or silver like it had been earlier that morning. Fred's aunty, Jess, who he lived with now (he didn't think of it as living, more as staying), was an illustrator. She had her own Derwents – Fred had looked at their names, and remembered being small and worried in his room.

He could see the forest ahead of them, beyond the cleared land. The Otways. Old growth, ancient trees. There must be a Forest Green? When he was a kid, Fred had been fascinated by all the different shades of one colour.

The bus stopped and started, lurching and braking more than usual. The regular driver was away and the new person was like an emergency teacher, who didn't know the kids, the ropes, the road.

They pulled over to the gravel edge to pick up more passengers. Kids going to the local high school, and others heading to the edge of the forest, to Otway Community School.

•

When they stopped at Lansborough, a little girl got on amongst a group of older kids. Fred didn't notice her, but Ash did. She looked too young for school. 'Do you reckon she's all right on her own?' Ash said to no one in particular, as Fred had his earbuds back in. 'I don't think the driver saw her get on.'

3

Ash stood up. Took out his buds. The bus swayed. He went over to her. She was sitting by herself, swinging her feet under the seat.

'Hey, what's your name?'

'Tessa.'

He sat down next to her. She was so small that her Bluey backpack fitted neatly beside her on a single seat.

'How old are you?'

The little girl held up five fingers proudly.

'Where are you going, Tessa?'

'To see my nanna.'

'Is she meeting you at the bus stop?'

'I'm going to her house.'

'On your own?'

She nodded confidently. 'Would you like some popcorn?'

Okay, maybe this was legit? 'No thanks, you have it.' The popcorn looked homemade. And fresh. When Tessa opened the bag, Ash could smell burnt butter.

'Do you go to school?'

'I'm going to Nanna's house today.'

'Right.'

Tessa seemed quite content, she was munching her popcorn from the small Glad bag on her lap. Like she was on an adventure for one. Swinging her little legs and her pink runners back and forward as the bus moved on. Maybe Ash was concerned for no reason.

'I like your runners,' he said.

'They're my new ones,' said Tessa, straightening her legs out in front of her. 'Nanna got them for me. She got them on her holiday.'

Tessa looked out the window.

After a few minutes, Ash went back to his seat beside Fred. 'We better keep an eye on that kid,' he said. 'She's only five and she's on her own.'

Fred shrugged. 'Not our responsibility, mate.'

Why not? Ash didn't get that thinking. And he wasn't sure about Fred yet, who seemed a bit angry or sarcastic or something, but they caught the bus together every day, and they'd been surfing a few times with some other guys. Fred was new to the school, and Ash liked to give everyone a go.

When they got off, Ash tossed up whether he should tell the bus driver to watch out for the little girl. But, you're not in the Kimberley now, he told himself. Not in the community, where everyone watches out for everyone. The driver might think he was weird. You could never tell. You had to be careful, these days, particularly if you were a guy taking interest in a little kid. The driver might have seen him go and sit with Tessa, might have already made a note of it. How sad is that, Ash thought, and he got that sick feeling when stuff in society really worried him, it was so wrong.

•

Chrystal woke with tinnitus roaring in her ears.

Elle wasn't in the sofa-bed against the wall. Chrystal heard the shower, and morning radio in the kitchen. Something about a weather warning, but she couldn't hear it properly, because the shower sound and the tinnitus sound mingled loudly in her head. What kind of weather warning? She didn't want bad weather when they were going on this camp or hike or whatever it was. They couldn't even take their phones. And she wouldn't like the food, she wouldn't be able to eat it. They wouldn't make her eat it, would they?

Elle came down the passageway to the bedroom, already dressed and putting her hair in a ponytail.

'Hey, Chrystal, we need to leave in twenty, you better get up.'

Elle didn't suggest a shower because Chrystal never seemed to have one. Elle watched her now, sitting up in bed, twirling her hair with one hand and clutching Snoopy, the stuffed toy she was obsessed with, in the other. She hadn't brought half the clothing on the exchange packing list but she'd brought this toy. Her hair fell on her shoulders in twisted strands. It was dirty.

'I have a headache,' she said dully.

'Do you want a Panadol?'

Chrystal acted as if she hadn't heard Elle. She did this all the time. Like she didn't know that if someone asks you a question you're supposed to answer it.

'It's because a storm is coming.'

'What?' said Elle from the doorway.

'I get a headache if a storm is coming,' said Chrystal, slowly getting out of bed.

That's kind of ridiculous, thought Elle, who had been patient for the past three weeks but was now sick of Chrystal.

Elle's dad was cooking pancakes in the kitchen. 'You'll need to fill up on these, girls.' He slipped them onto a plate. 'You have to carry your own food in, so best have a big breakfast.'

He held the plate to Chrystal. 'Pancake?'

Silence. Hands like incy-wincy spider.

'Chrystal?'

Chrystal picked up her phone. 'I guess.'

One thing that really got on Elle's nerves was that Chrystal never said please or thank you. She also never called Elle's parents by their names. And she never helped! She'd only offered one time, when she'd just got off the phone to her mum. 'Do you need help with the meal?' she'd said, too loudly, once dinner was already served. Elle thought that maybe Chrystal's mum had reminded her to say these things, ask these questions. Elle's own mum had said that they needed to be understanding, that maybe Chrystal was finding it stressful living with a family she didn't know. 'But she doesn't even clear her plate after dinner,' said Elle. It sounded petty, but it was so annoying! Couldn't she see the rest of the family picking their plates up and putting them in the dishwasher? It took like six seconds! 'And we've tried so hard!' Elle told her mum. 'You and Dad have, Hughie has, I have too.' Elle's dad had even asked if any of Chrystal's friends were also on the exchange program and if she'd like to see them. She didn't seem bothered.

Hughie, Elle's little brother, was chatting with their dad, but when the weather forecast came on the radio, Dad tilted his head, listening.

'Fine at first, but a severe weather warning with damaging wind, hail and heavy rain.'

'Do you reckon we'll still do the dropping, Dad?' Elle held her fork mid-air.

'I think so. Sounds like the worst of the weather won't hit us here until early tomorrow morning.' Butter spattered in the pan. 'You'll be back at school, safe and sound in your sleeping bags by then.' He slid another pancake onto Hughie's plate. 'And it's going to be a beautiful day today. A beautiful autumn day. Twenty-two degrees and sunny. Perfect!'

Elle went to the bench where her phone was charging, checked the weather app.

'You know we can't take our phones on the dropping.' She stopped. 'I should take a watch, so we'll know the time.'

'I think you get one phone for emergencies.' Dad sipped his coffee, leaning against the bench. His grey-green eyes matched the earthenware mug. 'They told us at the information evening. It might be worth taking a watch, though. Easier than digging a phone out of someone's backpack all the time.'

'I don't think I own a watch,' said Elle. 'Do you have one, Chrystal?'

'Hang on.' Dad put his mug on the bench. 'I have an old one you can use.'

He left the room.

'Do you have one?' Elle asked again. 'Chrystal? A watch?'

Chrystal didn't look up from her phone.

Elle rolled her eyes at Hughie.

'Here you go,' said Dad, handing Elle a digital watch. 'This one still works.'

'Thanks.' Elle played with the buttons. It was a Casio. A light, a stopwatch and an alarm. 'Water Resist,' she read the words across the watch's black plastic face. She smiled. 'You know these are cool again, Dad? They're vintage, from the eighties.' Elle pushed the button on the left-hand side again, the digits were dimly backlit – 7:43.

'Do you want one too, Chrystal? I reckon I could find another watch somewhere.'

Silence.

'Chrystal?'

She looked up from her phone, stared past Elle's dad vacantly. She hummed; she was always humming. It drove Elle crazy.

'Would you like to borrow a watch?'

'Mmmmmmm I don't wear one.'

'Do you want one for the dropping, though?'

'On account of the ticking.'

'Does the ticking bother you?'

No answer.

'This one's digital. No ticking.'

Chrystal went back to her manic texting. 'I don't wear one,' she repeated. Snoopy was wedged under her arm, her thumbs moving constantly, rapidly across her phone. What was she doing on it all day and night? Elle wondered, and what would she do when she couldn't have it for eight hours on the hike? There was supposed to be a rule at Elle's place – no phones at the table during mealtimes. But not having her phone seemed to make Chrystal so anxious that Elle's parents appeared to have made a silent exception for her.

Who was she messaging? Friends back home in America? She hadn't made any friends in the time she'd been here. Elle didn't think she'd made much of an effort. Like she didn't think she needed to, or didn't understand how to.

Everyone had said that having an exchange student was such a great experience, and Elle had thought it would be. She'd known people from all over the world, and had been looking forward to sharing these six weeks with a new friend. Someone who she might be friends with for life, even. Show her around where she lived now. The Otways. The Great Ocean Road. The Twelve Apostles, Loch Ard Gorge. People came from everywhere to see these places. And Elle made friends easily. Quickly. But it hadn't worked out that way.

They got their packs and put them in the boot of the car. Elle had had to lend Chrystal a lot of the gear. She was supposed to bring that stuff with her, but all she'd brought were shorts and t-shirts with the sleeves cut off. And Snoopy. Did she think that it's hot all the time in Australia? They have snow in Madison, where she lived, so it wasn't as if she'd never heard of warm clothes.

And she'd brought candy, as Chrystal called it. 'I didn't know if you'd have candy here,' she'd told Elle when Elle had asked why she had bags and bags of lollies in her suitcase. 'The candy I like.'

'Candy's basically sugar and food colouring, the world over,' said Elle. 'It tastes pretty much the same everywhere. Except in Sweden,' she added, 'where they have those rules about artificial colours and sweeteners.'

'What about Reese's Peanut Butter Cups, do you have them?'

'I think you can get them in some supermarkets. Not here, but in Melbourne.'

Elle knew about the properties of candy because she liked to bake. She liked following the steps of a recipe, even complicated recipes. She'd made hot cross buns just last weekend because of Easter, and thought Chrystal might like to help, but Chrystal had sat on her phone while Elle made the dough, the glaze, the gooey flour-and-oil combo for the cross.

Elle's mum had bought Chrystal some warm clothes – socks, a fleecy and a waterproof jacket – when she'd been in Melbourne for work, and Chrystal also had borrowed Elle's clothes. But they were such different shapes. Elle was tall with long legs, strong and muscular. Chrystal was small and fine, but fleshy, with pale skin.

She has such a bad diet, thought Elle, all she eats is lollies, no wonder she's so pale, and has no muscles. Elle was usually easygoing, but she was literally counting the days on her phone calendar until Chrystal would be flying back to America.

•

In the car on the way to school, they heard the severe weather warning again. Chrystal looked up from her phone. 'Is that storm where we're going?'

It was so rare for Chrystal to ask a question or contribute to any conversation that it almost gave Elle a fright when she did. 'It's for Cape Otway,' she reassured Chrystal, who was gripping Snoopy tightly so that he looked like he was being strangled. 'It's going the other way.'

It was hard to know how Chrystal was feeling when she spoke because it was always a monotone, all one level for every

11

word. As if her body, her voice, wasn't really connecting with the meaning of what she was saying.

'The worst you'll get is some rain,' said Elle's dad from the driver's seat. 'A bit of rain never hurt anyone. If we get really bad weather it'll be tomorrow morning, like I said. No need to worry, Chrystal! And who knows, it might just blow away out to sea. That's happened before.' Elle glimpsed her dad's face in the rear-view mirror, his eyes crinkling up as he smiled.

Elle wasn't worried because her dad wasn't worried. He turned right on the dirt road and headed up the hill to school. He parked, got out and helped them with their backpacks and jackets from the boot. 'Take care, look after yourselves,' he said and he gave Elle a hug, kissed the side of her head, his moustache tickling her. He put an arm around Chrystal too, an awkward side-hug, but she stood like a block of wood and looked straight ahead. 'Hughie, I'll pick you up at three. See you tomorrow, girls!'

They set off, but then her dad called Elle back.

'What? Did we forget something?'

'Look after her, won't you.' He nodded towards Chrystal, standing staring in the middle of the driveway.

'What?'

'Don't ignore her, this might be hard for her.'

'Yes, Dad, I'll look after her, okay?' Didn't he care that it was hard for Elle, too, to have this painful girl shadowing her all the time? At least her family got a break from Chrystal during the day. Elle had her all day at school as well. Twenty-four seven.

Otway Community School, or OCS, was a cluster of mud-brick, rounded buildings in a clearing at the end of the dirt road. It looked more like a retreat you'd see on Airbnb than a school. Nearly all the walls were curved, and the windows, too. Curved walls instil calm. Elle's friend Laila always said that. And whenever she said it, Laila put her hands out to touch those walls, as if she was getting energy from the warm bricks themselves; her long, slim, suntanned fingers spread out and still against the rammed earth.

Elle and Chrystal entered the main hall. Older kids were lounging on beanbags or in the conversation pit around the fireplace, while younger kids played outside. Wood was stacked for the fire that night when they'd be sleeping at school, after the dropping. Some kids had hot chocolate or chai they'd made in the kitchen, where you could go anytime you like and get a snack or whatever. The main hall was all timber and glass, with a tall cathedral ceiling.

The school didn't look like a regular school because it wasn't a regular school. But Elle hadn't ever really been to a regular school. She'd been to an international school in Hong Kong, one in Stockholm, and another in The Hague. And now here. Her parents moved around, so Elle and Hughie did too. It was because her mum worked for the Department of Foreign Affairs and Trade. DFAT, they called it. Even Elle didn't know exactly what her mum did there. Something to do with the attorney-general's office. Her parents wanted to move back to Australia before Elle started secondary school, so her mum got a transfer to a department involved in primary industry and exports. That's why they lived near Lavers Hill, because it was the part of Victoria where there was the dairy industry and the timber industry. Her dad was a music teacher; sometimes he worked and sometimes he didn't.

•

Chrystal sighed, sat on her pack, Snoopy on her lap, and kept snapchatting or messaging or whatever she was doing on her phone.

At first Elle had been embarrassed for Chrystal, who didn't seem to notice when people laughed at a fourteen-year-old carrying a soft toy around.

'How's your headache?'

'I have a headache,' Chrystal repeated as if no one had mentioned it before.

'Did you want the Panadol?'

No answer again. Elle handed her the little foil packet. Chrystal took it and put it in her pocket. Chrystal had a child's hands, small and white, but her fingernails were long – not manicured long, but uneven, dirty, not-cut long. Every time Elle saw them, she wanted to get the nail scissors and trim them back, one by one, neatly and evenly.

'Want me to get you some water so you can take them? The tablets?'

Chrystal took out some candy from her backpack.

Whatever, thought Elle. What was wrong with her? Was she homesick? Actually sick? Did she just hate Elle, and everything about Australia? Or was she like this all the time? Chrystal gave nothing away. The only part of her that moved were her thumbs on the phone, frantic. Elle peered over Chrystal's shoulder, but Chrystal hunched her back – she was an expert at hiding what was on the screen in her hand. She never mentioned any friends, so Elle was genuinely curious as to who she was communicating with non-stop. And she was texting even faster than usual, like it was a series of urgent messages, a warning.

Elle sat down beside her. 'Who are you messaging?'

Why did she even bother! Chrystal just behaved as if Elle hadn't spoken.

'Want a chai? Chrystal?'

Did her tinnitus actually stop her from hearing?

Elle made a chai for herself, and took one back to Chrystal. People drifted in, teachers and kids. None of Elle's friends had arrived, because the bus wasn't here yet. She looked out the thick, dappled glass to the sky, which was clear and blue. The air was crisp, but the chill would fade soon, she could feel the sun's gentle warmth through the glass already. There was no pollution here. Not like in Hong Kong.

There were also no bells at OCS, but at 8:45 they left their packs and wandered into morning group in the adjoining room. Another curved wood and glass space, warm timber floors, linen curtains swaying gently, the soft autumn morning flooding in through big square skylights in the ceiling. Someone was playing acoustic guitar.

Everyone was here now: Laila, the other kids who had exchange students with them, Ash and the new boy Fred. You weren't supposed to have phones in school, and every morning it was the same routine where one of the teachers quietly told Chrystal that phones were against the rules during school time. If it had been a local kid, they probably would have confiscated the phone but because these were exchange students who were allowed phones at their school in America, the teachers were more lenient with them.

'Our country, our rules,' Fred had said, laughing, but none of the OCS kids ever spoke like that.

After reflections and notices, the head teacher Johan read out the names of each group for the dropping later that day. There was a feeling of excitement in the air. Four groups would go by bus out into the forest. When Johan read out Elle's name, she hoped that Chrystal's wouldn't follow. In a group, the mood of one person could wreck everything. 'Upset the dynamic energy' is the way Laila would describe it. Laila's name was next to be read out, which made Elle happy, because Laila was the best, and also, nothing really bothered her. Which would be good on a night-time hike. Next name – Chrystal Diebert. Oh well, I was expecting that, thought Elle. At least I've got Laila. The last two in their group were Ash and Fred. Elle liked Ash, and Fred was new, so it would be a good opportunity to get to know him. At the other schools Elle had been to, kids came and went all the time, so you got used to making friends pretty quickly. An average posting of DFAT families was three years, before moving on again.

Chrystal went up to Johan. She looked tiny standing beside him. 'When's the storm coming?' she asked, too loudly. She clutched Snoopy, squashed under her arm.

Johan looked surprised; it was probably the first time Chrystal had spoken to him. 'There's some weather forecast for Cape Otway,' he said. 'You might get rain but nothing

16

too dramatic, Chrystal. Everyone should have a weatherproof jacket. Do you have one?'

Chrystal ignored him and went over to Sammi, the other head teacher. 'When's the storm coming?' she repeated in the same monotonal voice.

Can she shut up about the storm, thought Elle. They've already told us that it'll only be rain. And the whole point of a dropping is that it's supposed to be a challenge. It's not meant to be easy.

Chrystal came back to the group. Elle could feel her standing too close. When she stood with you, she was either too far away, an awkward distance, or too near, invading your personal space with the odd humming that she did before she spoke. Elle turned the other way. But Chrystal yanked on her sleeve and addressed the question to Elle's shoulder.

'When's the storm coming?'

•

Tessa got off the bus when she saw the red fence. She had been on the bus for a long time, longer than it took to get to Nanna's when she went with Mum.

She counted the posts of the fence. She knew there were twenty-four before the gate. She could count to one hundred now that she had started school. Twenty-two, twenty-three, twenty-four, twenty-five, twenty-six, twenty-seven . . . ouch! Now she had a splinter.

Where was the gate?

Tessa stopped.

Where was the shop with the daisies on the curtains?

Where was the park with the wooden fort?

Tessa couldn't even see the beach.

She turned around and walked the other way. There was a big green sign but Tessa couldn't read everything yet. She was only in prep. Did it say Apollo Bay? Where Nanna lived?

She walked along the gravel beside the road. She pushed at the splinter, but it hurt, and it wouldn't come out.

This wasn't like yesterday, when Mum took her on the bus to Nanna's on her way to work. When she'd had a sniffle and Mum said she could go to Nanna's for the day instead of school.

Now there was only a little bit of popcorn left.

Tessa looked up at the sky, the fluffy clouds.

She wanted her mum, her nanna.

Where was she?

Two

In English class, Fred stared out the window. The sky was Sky Blue; the forest, Forest Green. Fred daydreamed through the colours. As well as Pink Madder Lake, wasn't there a Rose Madder Lake? Fred smiled to himself, like a lake was mad and just got madder. Or Rose Madder could be a name, a girl's name.

The lesson, the whole day, dragged for Fred, probably for all the Year Nines because they were excited to get going on the dropping.

Kids didn't always work in their year levels at OCS, and after English, Fred was given the task of chopping wood with a group of Year Fives.

'What happens if they stuff it up?' he asked Johan.

'You're the instructor, Fred,' said Johan, 'not me.'

Johan always spoke like this. Open-ended. At Fred's last school everything was an instruction, and a punishment. Consequences for your Actions. Do this or you'll get a detention. Do that or an email will go to your parents. A PBR. Positive Behaviour Reminder. Teacher-speak for 'Your kid's a pain in the neck'. Kids called it your Personal Bullshit Record.

Two PBRs equals an email sent home. Three PBRs equals one detention.

Anyway, it turned out Fred didn't need to tell the Year Fives much at all, most of them knew how to chop wood better than he did. He who'd never had to do it before. Well, only once. He didn't want them to notice that he was learning from watching them. Year Fives. Embarrassing. Maybe Johan knew that would happen anyway.

'Hey, do they check our bags before we go on the dropping?' Fred asked Ash at lunchtime.

'No,' said Ash, 'they trust us.'

•

Elle, Laila and some others ate their lunch sitting in the sunshine on the big flat rocks by the creek at the bottom of the property. Elle's dad had been right, the weather was perfect. It was hard to believe that it would rain later like the forecast said. But then weather in the Otways was so changeable. You could go for one walk and need a fleecy, a slicker, a t-shirt, hat and sunscreen.

Water sparkled as it tumbled over the stones. Insects sat on the surface, and every now and then, shadows of fish moved underneath. 'Look at that!' said Elle as a couple of fish came up out of the water, jumping around. 'I've never seen that before, except in China when people are feeding the carp.'

'They're eating those insects on the water,' said Ash. 'Check it out, Chrystal!' Ash tried to engage her. Chrystal sat with them but it was as if she wasn't there.

At one o'clock it was Laila's yoga class. If people had a particular talent or interest, they could run a lunchtime club. Elle ran a baking class one day a week, their friend Simone had a running group, and there was a book club, music groups, taekwondo, painting, chess, woodwork, and other things. Everyone called Laila's class Junior Guru, because her dad was an actual guru. Laila's family lived in a treehouse.

Elle helped Laila set up the mats in the main hall. Laila was so graceful; she even unrolled her yoga mat like it was an elegant dance move. Elle felt lucky to know Laila. In the past, if Elle had a best friend at school, sooner or later their family would pack up and leave, or Elle and her family would leave. It always hurt. Elle had learnt to keep a part of herself to herself. For her own protection. Laila was as close to a best friend as Elle would let herself have.

Laila lit the candles and put her bag of stones on the raised area in front of the fireplace. The light softened, Elle smelt the woody, sweet scent.

Chrystal was sitting on a beanbag on her phone (against the rules) in the open area of the main hall. Better go through the motions, Elle thought, remembering her dad's words about not ignoring Chrystal. 'Do you want to do yoga with us?' she asked. Chrystal didn't even look up, just continued her high-speed texting.

Everyone said Elle could run any club, because she was what people called 'an all-rounder'. She could bake, she could run a half marathon, she could sew, she could build a vegetable garden, play piano, she could paint a room, she could make jewellery. She even knew how to wire up lights, she'd done that when they had a party in the barn in the school paddock. She got good marks, too. So it annoyed her that she found getting along with Chrystal so difficult. Elle had met people who were different in all sorts of ways, but she'd never had to live with them, look after them, figure them out.

Elle decided to put Chrystal out of her mind. She went and found a mat, took off her shoes, re-tied her hair and sat cross-legged, ready.

About fifteen kids and a couple of teachers were in the class.

Ash and Fred appeared at the door. Elle watched Ash. She liked his smile, his loping walk. Like now, coming in, wearing loose trackies, his long hair halfway between ringlets and dreadlocks. His body swayed with each step, he pulled his hoodie off up over his shoulders in one movement. His worn t-shirt came up with the hoodie, showing his six-pack. His shoulder muscles moved, ripples under his smooth skin, as he took down a mat from the pile on the wooden shelves. Fred stayed at the door. He wasn't tall like Ash, his hair was short and cropped, he stood, small and still and hardened, like his whole body was ungiving somehow.

Ash put his mat beside Elle's, then went back to get the wooden blocks and blanket. 'Are you coming in?' he asked Fred. 'Want to do it?'

'Nah.' Fred leant against the wall. 'I'll stay here though, to watch her.'

'Laila?'

Fred smiled. 'Yeah. She's loony, but she's hot.'

Ash knew you were supposed to call your mates out when they said stuff like this. Or was this allowed? Were you allowed to say someone was hot? Who knew?

'I like Laila.' Was that a supportive comment?

'I know you do.' Fred shoved Ash in a friendly way.

'No, I mean she's a friend. She used to go out with that guy.' Ash pointed across the room. 'Joe, Year Ten. But they broke up.' Everyone had heard the rumours that Joe had treated Laila badly. Ash wasn't in Elle and Laila's close friendship group, but he still considered them friends. Ash was friends with everyone.

'I know people think she's a bit la-la-land,' said Ash, 'but look at her, she does seem really, like, calm. You know her dad is Griffin Moss? He's world famous. A guru. He can heal people.'

'Yeah but he's not a proper doctor,' said Fred. 'My dad did twelve years at uni to be a psychiatrist.'

Laila was sitting on the floor of the low stage, in front of the fireplace, about to start. Ash thought she looked beautiful, the way the candlelight fell on the side of her face like that, the soles of her feet in their stripy wool socks together as if it was the most comfortable way to sit. Eyes closed, her back and shoulders straight, but also relaxed.

Ash went back to his mat. Fred stayed where he was.

Laila put on some soft music, bell chimes. She began to speak.

'I'm going to take you through the chakras, the energy centres in your body. This was taught to me by my father,' she continued in a slow, almost musical voice, 'whom I admire deeply.' She sounded formal, but flowing, as if she were reciting a poem.

23

Okay so this chick's in love with her father, clearly, thought Fred. Still, it was like a lullaby, or being hypnotised or something. Listening to that voice, and the chimes. Smelling the wood smoke and something sweet. The sun sliding in through the window. Fred felt his shoulders, his neck relax. Closed his eyes, just for a moment. Listened to Laila's instructions about deep breathing. All other sound around him fell away . . .

A clatter in the kitchen jolted Fred. He opened his eyes and looked across to Ash, doing some kind of warrior stance. Fred didn't know Ash well, he didn't know any of them well, but he wished he could be a bit more like Ash. A bit more chilled. But how could Fred be what he wanted to be? Maybe he should have done the yoga. Ash looked pretty unco. He was a fit guy who surfed and played footy, but he wasn't very . . . Fred tried to find a word . . . graceful. Not many guys were flexible. Elle was good, but Laila was different altogether. She was bending backwards and her loose t-shirt fell, so Fred could see her flat tummy. Her long hair, the colour of honey, tumbling in its loose bun, down over her shoulders. She was so supple, she morphed from one pose to the next, like her body was liquid.

Fred would have liked to try it, but he hated being the worst at something. The worst in the class. Jess said that the Moss Yoga Retreat was famous. She'd been to some of Griffin Moss's workshops. Fred felt a bit obvious standing in the doorway, but he didn't know where to go. This school was so different from others he'd been to, where you just went where you were told. He checked his phone, even though it wasn't allowed. A message from Jess, saying sorry she'd missed him that morning, and have a good time. Nothing from his mum, or his dad.

Fred looked around to see if there were any Year Nines he could go and stand with. But there was only that weirdo Chrystal nearby with a couple of other exchange students. They hadn't joined the Junior Guru class either.

Laila was taking some gemstones from a cloth drawstring bag. 'Choose a stone to hold if you like. Black tourmaline will release negative energy in your body. This stone also serves for protection. Hematite will push away the dark moods of others by reconnecting your spirit to the energy of the Earth.' She went on, describing each stone and placing them on the floor in front of her. 'Amethyst can relieve stress and provide balance. Moonstone, for support when you're feeling out of touch,' she paused, 'with your feelings.'

Fred scoffed. He could see Ash, taking it all seriously.

Chrystal had moved a bit closer to him, watching, too.

Fred could hear her humming.

'Not into crystals, Chrystal?' Fred said.

'Mmmmmmmm I'm not a crystal.'

'Yeah, I know that.' Jesus, thought Fred, I'm surrounded by loons.

'I have an H.'

'What?'

'C-H-R-Y-S-T-A-L.' She spelt her name out. She spoke like a robot.

'Yeah, whatever. I didn't think you were an actual crystal, Chrystal.' They watched everyone choose a stone. 'Have you done yoga?' Fred asked her.

Chrystal had tried yoga. She knew she was no good at it. She couldn't even do child's pose, or the downward dog. It made her feel wrong, in her body.

'I can't do it, on account of my ankle.'

Humming again. What was with the humming?

'What's wrong with your ankle?'

Doesn't answer. Talks to Snoopy. Walks off.

Fred watched her. She did walk in a strange way – was that because of her ankle, or because she was a total nutcase? And what's with the Snoopy toy?

He turned back to Laila and the class. Now they were all lying down with their eyes closed. It made Fred feel stressed, annoyed suddenly. He turned to walk away.

'Hey, Chrystal,' he called back, 'want to see where you can use your phone and they won't find you?'

'Sure.' She said the word in an odd way, too upbeat, as if she'd been told to emphasise the wrong part of it.

Chrystal followed Fred down behind the main building beside the water tanks. 'No one ever comes down here,' he said.

They stood with their phones. There were a couple of other kids there, and some older students, maybe Year Twelve. One of them was smoking a rollie.

Fred felt embarrassed now, being there with this bizarre girl humming non-stop with a Snoopy under her arm. He wanted to tell the others she wasn't his friend. He wondered if they'd hassle them, but they seemed chilled, just carried on texting and smoking.

'Can you stop that humming?'

'There's going to be a storm,' Chrystal said in her robot voice.

'Are you on the weather app?' Fred looked over to her phone which she held so he couldn't see.

She didn't answer, so he said, 'You know we can't take our phones on the dropping?'

Then he realised that, without a phone, they wouldn't know the time. He hoped someone in his group would have a watch. He had one, but it was broken. Fred felt his neck tense when he pictured it. On the first day of this new school, he had thrown his watch out the window of the bus when he got on at Kennett River. He knew the tyres had crushed it, because each morning at the bus stop he could see it in the gutter, broken. It felt good that the watch was still there, crushed and smashed in the face. Only he knew its story, that it had been his. It gave Fred a tight feeling all the way up from his legs, but at the same time made him feel triumphant. He could see it each morning, getting more wrecked and less recognisable as a watch. His watch, a gift. Yeah, it made Fred feel good. Stuff his dad. Stuff time. His father had given him a watch because it was a joke that Fred was never on time, never stuck to a schedule. As if a stupid, expensive watch would change that. As if he'd wear it. He didn't even like it, it wasn't his style. It wasn't a gift, it was a message, an instruction.

Fred got back to the main room just as yoga was finishing. It smelt like vanilla, or cinnamon or something. The timber was the colour of caramel. Soft music. Soft lighting. Soft furniture. Soft warmth. Fred felt like turning up the lights, shouting at them, 'Wake up!' Imagine if he had! Probably get you expelled in a place like this. Or maybe they'd send him to a psychiatrist. His dad. lol.

People were slowly sitting up from their final relaxation. Some looked a bit dazed, as if they'd been transported some-where else, hypnotised maybe, and were coming out of a trance.

'Try to bring this calm, centred feeling into the rest of your day.' Laila put her hands together like a prayer, or forgiveness, nodding. 'Namaste.'

A couple of kids had actually gone to sleep. Fred felt his tummy clench. He couldn't look at them, but couldn't look away.

Laila stood up without putting her hands on the floor. She picked up the stones from each person's spot and put them back in her bag. She laid a hand gently on the shoulders of people still sleeping, waking them.

Fred went over to Ash as he was packing up his mat. He picked up one of the stones. 'Do you buy these online?' he called loudly to Laila, breaking the spell of the room. 'The stones?'

Laila looked up. 'I found some of them, the rest I was given, from my father.'

'Whom I admire deeply,' sniggered Fred, hoping Ash would hear, respond, laugh.

'Is he a geologist or something?' Fred knew who he was, but he wanted to hear how Laila described her father.

'No, he's a . . . teacher.' Laila continued collecting the stones, dropping them into her bag where they clinked together.

She probably only thought calm, healing thoughts. Fred rolled his eyes. But then how would it be to really admire your father. He let himself imagine that, just for a moment. It'd make your life so much easier, like you had a path to follow, or something.

As the others were putting the mats away, Fred slipped the black tourmaline into his pocket. Later, in class, he took it out, turned the stone in his hand. It was cool and smooth. Black, like the name said, but Fred could see lots of colours. There was a bit of blue in there, too. Some very dark brown. It warmed up as he held it. Ivory Black. Indigo. What were the names of the browns? When his mum had renovated her kitchen, she called the colour of the new stone bench 'charcoal', but Fred had stared at that bench so often that the tiny specks of stone became individual pieces of colour, like the Seurat print in Jess's studio. Ivory Black, Blue Grey, Gunmetal, French Grey. Silver Grey. The dots made him stressed, as if he couldn't see the whole, like literally couldn't join those dots so that they meant anything. Then when he switched focus, the bench was just one colour again. Like his mum said. Charcoal.

One of the last times he'd sat at that bench, stared at its pixelated colours, was when he was home from boarding school for the holidays last year. Could have been the last time he really did try to talk to someone. He'd wanted to say that he felt bad, ashamed, that he'd done something he'd regretted. That he couldn't bear to go back to that school. But his mum had said it was late and they'd talk in the morning, and then he'd looked at the colours and they'd all swum together. In the morning, she'd already left for work.

She didn't want Fred, didn't want him to be honest with her, so he protected her from himself, closed up, clicked shut like the lid of a tin of Derwents.

•

At Ferntree Primary School, the front office staff were busy collecting notices for the book fair. The list of absentees came in. Tessa L from Prep S. She'd been absent yesterday as well. Had the parents phoned in? The receptionist made a note to call the family and check.

•

At two pm, Johan gathered the Year Nines in the assembly area and went over the plans one last time. Kids sat around on the cushioned benches under the tall windows that faced the forest.

Johan was Dutch, and the dropping was a Dutch activity. Whenever parents complained about activities Johan had adapted from Dutch education, he told them that a UNICEF report found that Dutch children are the happiest in the world. So maybe Johan did have some idea of what he was doing. When Elle had lived in The Hague, her Dutch friends had told her about droppings. It was a tradition there. Every kid did it – at school, or scouts, or in family groups. Elle had only been there for a year; it had been during the height of social distancing so they'd had no camps or anything like that.

'So, you know the arrangement. We drop you in the forest at four pm, and you must find your way back to school by midnight,' he told the group.

'Yeah, you've told us that,' said Fred, who was still getting used to the fact that you could talk back to teachers at this school. They said you could talk to a teacher as if everyone was equal. And you actually could.

Some kids were excited, some nervous, and some, like Chrystal, were getting in the last of their tech time before phones would be taken away. There were no uniforms at OCS, so the assembly area was a sea of colour, bright knitted scarves and beanies, hoodies, striped leggings.

'There will be ten red buckets to follow,' said Johan. 'They will each have notes in them with minimal instruction.'

Ten red buckets, thought Fred. It sounded like a nursery rhyme. Ten green bottles.

'What happens if we go the wrong way?' he called out.

'There will be buckets at any major dead ends too, so you'll know, and you can backtrack,' said Sammi. 'Each group will have a map, a first-aid kit, a compass and five head torches. These items are your best friend on a dropping. Each group will also have a phone with one number for use in absolute emergencies only. So don't worry, you'll be able to access an adult if you really need to.'

'We won't be doing that,' Fred called out. 'Who would ever want to access an adult!'

'The most important thing is to stay with your group,' said Sammi. They had already done practical exercises, like orienteering and compass-reading, been on trial hikes, and emails had been sent to the families about resilience, teamwork and staying calm under pressure.

'You know to wear your high-vis vests, and stay together over the twenty-seven kilometres,' added Johan. He clapped his big hands, all excited about his dropping idea. 'It's a full moon tonight, a supermoon! A beautiful night for an adventure. Enjoy yourselves, enjoy the challenge. And look after each other!'

Everyone picked up their packs. 'Twenty-seven ks!' moaned Fred. 'This is going to be the worst.'

'Oh, one last thing.' Some kids sat down again, sighed. 'A couple of you have expressed concern about the weather,' said Johan. 'There is a severe weather warning, but it won't reach this area until early tomorrow morning, by which time you'll be back at school asleep by the fire here. Part of your time it will be very pleasant, sunny, and later you might get a bit wet but that's all. You should all have your waterproof jacket and boots.'

Chrystal had insisted on wearing her cheap runners, even though Elle's mum had bought her the Gore-Tex ones. 'You'll get wet feet,' Elle had told her, 'will you be okay with that?' Elle wondered now whether she should point it out to Johan, but he was big on people taking personal responsibility for their decisions.

'Enough with the preparation already!' said Fred as he swung his backpack across his shoulders. They made their way outside to the waiting bus.

Fred looked up at the sky. Still blue, Sky Blue. Sunshine lit up the puffy clouds. So white, they were dazzling. One looked like a mushroom. The air was warm. Fred was even sweating a bit. Everyone just wanted to get going, now.

•

Tessa kept walking. Her feet hurt. Her new runners had made a blister on the back of her heel. And the pink was getting all dirty. She was hot in her jacket. And she still had the splinter. Where was the beach? It was the wrong way! A big bus went past and gave her a fright. It was too noisy. 'I want that bus to stop,' said Tessa out loud to herself, watching it become smaller as it got further away from her. That bus could take me home, but now it's gone. How can I find another bus?

She was so tired she thought she might cry.

Tessa's feet were very sore, so she sat down under a big tree on the side of the road, and took off her shoes. Her heel was red and the blister still hurt. No blood though, Tessa didn't like blood at all.

Three

The bus set off at three pm. Some kids up the back were singing, but most were on their phones, earbuds in.

Ash and Fred sat near the back, with Elle and Laila in front of them, and Chrystal across the aisle with Bree, one of the other exchange students. Chrystal wore wide brown sunglasses, thick at the sides, that looked too big for her face.

Fred had a window seat. Even if he didn't want to, he noticed things. Slanted sunlight shone in pale shafts through the trees and across the road. Like a path to the sky. Spectrum Orange. Naples Yellow. Sometimes Fred didn't hear what people said because he was in a kind of daze, looking at something or other. A colour. But sometimes it was helpful to notice things. If he wanted to, Fred could remember stuff by recalling what it looked like. Even sentences. Sometimes paragraphs. It helped if he ever felt like trying at anything.

Australian forests weren't that bright, clear, translucent green that you see in storybooks. They were olive, grey, wild. Was there a colour called Wild Green? If there was, it would be the colour of an Australian forest.

Ash tapped Elle's shoulder. 'Hey, what snacks did you bring?'

Elle turned around. 'Fruit, sandwiches, chocolate, not that much though, you know we have to carry everything.'

'Did you bring those cookies you made when we did bake club?'

Elle nodded. 'And half a mud cake.' Everyone had loved those cookies. Chrystal wouldn't eat them though. She would eat cookie dough but not cookies.

'I bought some of the dough for you, Chrystal.'

Elle turned back to Ash. 'She only eats soft food.'

'Right.'

'That's right, isn't it, Chrystal? Only soft food? And mostly white. Pasta, bread, pancakes, cheese?'

'But not the cheese you have here,' Chrystal said from across the aisle. 'Mac and cheese.'

Yes, said Elle to herself, turning away from Chrystal, I know you don't like the cheese we have here. You've told me that one hundred times. Elle gritted her teeth. She was supposed to go to America at the end of the year because it was a reciprocal exchange! She'd have to get out of that, somehow. No way was she going to spend six more weeks living with Chrystal.

The bus had circled up a mountain and was coming down the other side.

'We're going a long way from school.' Fred sighed. He hated bushwalking. He knew Ash was looking forward to it; the national parks had all been closed for so long because of the bushfires, and then the virus. At boarding school, Fred had been sent home for a term, had to do online learning. He'd thought it might be a bit like a holiday, but it was just a battle every day between him, his mum, his phone and his PlayStation. Then he went back, and all the trouble happened. And his mum had the great idea of farming him off to her sister Jess.

Afternoon sun reflected off the road signs. It caught on the bark of trees, sharpening textures and colour. Leaves glinted. Then, just like that, the sun was behind the hill and the world was suddenly Water Green, Sap Green, Silver Grey. The whole colour of the forest became darker. Duller. Fred put on his music. The last time he'd been in the bush was with his dad when they went on a totally awkward bushwalk. It was the day Fred was told that he'd be packed off to boarding school. After the walk, they were splitting wood for the woodpile at Louise's holiday house in the country, near Castlemaine. Fred had never done that before, and he'd never seen his father do it either. It was kind of funny, his dad pretending to be this physical he-man chopping wood and stuff, when that so wasn't his dad at all. It's like he'd looked at some clinical notes – *Fathers should spend time with their sons doing something physical. Chopping wood is one such activity. Try chopping wood.*

When his dad had said on that day, 'How about boarding school?' Fred knew it wasn't 'how about', it was 'you're going'. He'd felt his heartbeat, something quicken in his chest. But he'd nodded, said yeah that'd be fine, yes, Dad, a good experience, and yes, I reckon Bellarine would be good, even though it's two hours from where you live. Yeah they have surf camps, it'll be fine, I'll be fine.

'Of course we'll miss you,' his dad had said, looking at the wood, and Fred had felt like screaming at him, 'Do you think

36

I'm some kind of idiot? If you thought you'd miss me you wouldn't be sending me to boarding school. You're relieved that I won't be here to muck up your new life.' But Fred had kept nodding and chopping the wood. After a while, his dad went in for a coffee or whatever, and forgot about chopping wood then. He'd said what he needed to say. But Fred didn't go inside. Fred kept breaking it up, slamming the axe down, not doing it the way his dad had tried to teach him, his earbuds in now, Violent Soho turned up as loud as it would go, all that split wood, until Louise came home much later and said, 'Fred, what are you doing?'

Fred took his buds out, looked down at his hands. They were bleeding. He was so scared. He didn't even know where he was, where he'd been, what had happened.

That was how his dad gave him the name blind Freddy. 'Couldn't you see what you were doing?' he said.

Couldn't *you*? thought Fred.

'Look at the blisters on your hands, and cuts from the timber. Splinters, too. What are you, mate, blind Freddy?' It was some stupid saying. Fred looked it up. Someone who has little perception.

Fred *could* see. He could see heaps of things. All those Derwent colours, in his head, in his eyes.

The bus went up and down another steep hill. Ahead of them was the mountain range. A band of cloud sat just above it, like a long, grey shelf. The trees were taller now, which made the winding road seem narrow. The edge dropped to a steep gully with tree ferns and mountain ash trees rising up out of it. The ferns had mossy trunks, they looked prehistoric. Fred could almost imagine a dinosaur appearing on the road in front of them.

Some people were studying where the bus was going and making their own maps in notebooks. Chrystal leant against the window. Her tinnitus was getting worse. She turned her head left and then right, and the sound moved from one ear to the other, louder and quieter, like a magic trick that only she could hear. She turned her head again, looked out the window. Was that a little kid, between the trees? Kids probably went into the bush on their own, here in Australia. It was that kind of place. Her headache hadn't stopped. She took out her water bottle and swallowed the painkillers Elle had given her. Had she remembered to thank Elle? Should she thank her now? Her head throbbed more.

Eventually the bus pulled over to the side of the road. Kids jumped up. 'Are we here?' asked Laila.

Fred noticed a big white Hilux behind the bus, with a roo bar, a grille and spotlights. It looked like a face, the grimacing emoji.

'Not yet.' Johan unzipped a large bag. 'Everyone put one of these on for the last part of the trip.'

'You didn't tell us we'd be blindfolded!'

'Just for the final fifteen minutes.' He walked up the aisle of the bus, handing out blindfolds.

The Hilux accelerated and roared past them. Ash saw two big dogs in the back. One was pulling on a chain, barking. Ash felt heat rise in his body. He'd been bitten by a camp dog in the Kimberley and now he didn't trust them.

'They do this in Holland,' said Elle as she pulled the blind-fold down over her eyes and adjusted the elastic. 'To make it more challenging, disorientate people more.'

Fred tilted his head back and peered through the bottom of his blindfold. Elle and Ash were sitting obediently with theirs on. Laila, too. Suckers. Chrystal hadn't put hers on at all. She was still wearing those huge sunnies. Like someone from the 1960s. Roy Orbison or someone. It was like she didn't do anything unless you told her three times. She was so . . . slug-gish. She didn't seem like a rebel, more someone who couldn't bring herself to do anything. Fred wondered if anything would get Chrystal excited, or even just a bit animated. And that ridiculous toy she carried everywhere. Some people were just sitting ducks.

Everyone was trying to work out where they were. With her blindfold on, Elle heard snippets of conversation. When you lost one sense, the others compensated. That was a thing, wasn't it? Elle definitely thought her hearing was sharper once she was wearing a blindfold.

'Hang on, are we going down again?'

'We turned right then, didn't we?'

'We're going across the ridge, along Dentons Road?'

'No, it's Beacon Ridge, I reckon.'

After a few minutes, they all became quiet, everyone aware and listening, focusing on the senses they could still use. Elle could hear Laila's steady breathing beside her. Laila reached out and rested her hand on Elle's forearm, making Elle's own breathing slow down.

The bus bounced over the rutted gravel road. Jolted. Revved, skidded a bit on the turns. Finally it came to a stop. There was no sound of the sea, or any other cars or engines. 'You can take your blindfolds off,' said Johan. 'Welcome to the deep, dark wood.' He laughed.

No Australian would describe it like that, thought Elle. For a start, no Australian forest is ever called the wood. That's for gentler forests, in other places, like Holland. Forests of a different scale, where the light is soft and the ground is mossy and feels like thick carpet. Small forests, with pretty trees, delicate leaves. Fields of lilies, poppies, violets. In Australian forests, the gum leaves are tough and don't rot on the ground. The trees shed bark and hard, sharp gumnuts. And you don't see gum trees lining avenues in cities, even Australian cities. Too rough, too asymmetrical, too big, too wild. Still, sometimes when she was running in the forest and allowed herself to stop still for a minute, it reminded Elle of being in a cathedral, like Notre Dame, or that one in Copenhagen. Grundtvig's Church. Which was strange because a cathedral is so ordered, so obviously a built structure. Yet the forest sometimes gave Elle the same feeling of being filled up with something she couldn't explain.

Everyone poured out and around to the side of the bus to get their packs. They were in a clearing, with towering trees overhead. Ash could smell eucalyptus – the messmate and the mountain ash. It was quiet except for the call of currawongs.

Johan handed around a basket for people to put their phones in. It reminded Elle of assemblies at her old school in Hong Kong, where they'd pass around a bowl and people would put a donation in for a charity. Like in church. An offering. Chrystal passed the basket on, as if she didn't have anything to give. When they were walking over to where Sammi was organising the groups, Johan stopped Chrystal. He was like this. You thought he didn't notice things, but he did. 'I need your phone, please, Chrystal,' he said, and held out his hand.

Chrystal stopped. It was hard to know where she was looking because of her sunglasses.

Elle stopped too.

'Mmmmmmmmm I thought because I'm on exchange –' said Chrystal.

'When you're at OCS, you need to respect our rules. No phone on any camps or outdoor activities, except as authorised by the staff.'

Johan kept his hand held out.

Chrystal stood there.

'You need to give him your phone,' Elle said, gently. 'You'll get it back later tonight.'

Chrystal slowly placed the phone in Johan's hand.

'Thank you, Chrystal, I'll return it to you at school.' Johan faced the group. 'I'm trusting that none of you is carrying a phone.'

Chrystal rubbed her hands together. Turned them, twisted them, one gripping the other like she was washing her hands in the air. Elle felt a pang of sympathy, or something. 'Chrystal,' she said, reaching out to her. 'Don't be stressed, it's just a hike.'

It was cooler in the forest. Some kids were already putting on hoodies. People were asking each other if they recognised the spot, if they'd been there before. 'It looks like the Triplet Falls picnic area, but it's not,' said Ash. 'What do you reckon, Laila?'

'I don't know it,' said Laila, looking around in a circle. She wore a red and purple loose woollen beanie with long sides that ended in thick tassels.

They must be in a remote part of the forest if even Laila wasn't sure where they were. She had lived in the area her whole life and knew it pretty well.

Johan told them to stand in their groups. Ash lifted his pack and Fred's to move them over to the others.

Fred's pack was heavy. 'What have you got in here?' Ash asked.

Fred smiled, and unzipped it to reveal a plastic bag with Smirnoff cans, Double Black.

'What do you want to bring that for?' said Ash.

'It'll be fun. Party in the forest.'

'We have to keep focused,' said Elle. 'We're going to be hiking, not sitting around drinking. We've only got a few hours.' She pointed at his bag. 'That'll be too heavy.'

'We can drink it early then,' said Fred. 'As soon as we're out of sight.'

'You shouldn't bring it. Leave it in the bus,' said Elle.

'They said it's not a race,' said Fred. 'Who cares if we stop for a bit?'

'We don't need that to enjoy nature,' said Laila, and Fred looked at her as if she was mad.

'Looks like I scored the lame group,' he said. 'I'm sure I can find some other kids who'll party with me. It's not like it's going to be hard to find our way out anyway. Just use the phone they give us!'

'It doesn't have Google Maps on it. It's only got the one number,' said Elle.

'Then we find a road and walk out.'

'Back home, the legal drinking age is twenty-one,' Chrystal said suddenly.

'Wow, she actually speaks!' said Fred, which was mean because he had spoken with her earlier that day, quite a bit actually. He had even acted as if he might have liked to be her friend.

'Yeah,' said Ash, 'but you can drive when you're sixteen!'

Fred zipped his backpack up. 'We can drink at eighteen, here.'

'Yeah, and you're fourteen, Fred,' said Ash, trying to make it light, non-threatening.

Fred shrugged and lifted his heavy bag onto his shoulders. His body was tense, wiry.

Why are people so obsessed with drinking? thought Elle. So much of her friends' conversation was about how they were going to get UDLs, where and when they were going to drink them, who had money, whose older brother or sister could get it, who could get some from home without their parents noticing, where they'd stash it. It seemed to occupy so much of their thinking. And it was really expensive. And boring for her when everyone just wanted to get drunk all the time.

Johan was standing, addressing the whole group. 'We expect you all back at school around midnight. Like I've said, it's not a race, so there's no need to rush or make hasty decisions. You can stop and eat your snacks as we discussed in the preparation classes. You can take a rest. It should take you approximately eight hours. You will all have head torches, and one phone per group to check the time, and for absolute emergencies. The lights will be on at school, and we'll be there with the fire going, hot chocolate and toasties.' He paused. 'There is light rain forecast so be prepared to be walking on slippery surfaces.'

'Rain!' someone groaned. But Johan said, 'Listen, it's just a walk in the dark. That's all it is. A walk in the dark! And it won't even be completely dark, because of the supermoon. Too easy for you. A supermoon is thirty per cent brighter than a regular full moon. Now, can one member of each group come and get your phone, map, compass and torches. Also your first-aid kit.'

Fred went and grabbed the stuff for their group, and immediately checked the phone to see what was on it. Could they get Google Maps?

Everyone put on their high-vis vests. Laila had her own style, she always had a long scarf that she wore draped around her neck, sometimes her head, her hair, sometimes her shoulders.

'I think we've covered everything back at school in the prep sessions,' said Johan. 'Any last questions?'

'Jesus, talk about overkill,' muttered Fred, next to Ash. 'You'll share the Double Blacks with me, won't you? Once we get going?'

Ash knew Fred wanted him to agree. Ash smiled weakly, half nodding and half shaking his head, and looked away.

Sammi took a step forward.

'Wait for it, here comes a team-building activity,' Ash said quietly. They all knew that Sammi loved this kind of thing.

'Without speaking, I want you to stand in your group and link arms so that you form a circle.'

'I knew it.' Ash smiled.

'This is your bond,' Sammi continued. 'You will need it to make the trip fun and get back safely. To stay connected.'

Elle noticed that other groups did this effortlessly. They formed the circle first and then linked arms. But hers didn't do it like that. She linked arms with Laila, then Ash joined them, but Fred groaned and Chrystal stood there like a sack of something heavy. Static. Except for her humming, like a toneless electrical noise, her own personal power station, and her hands, her fingers, which were pulling at Snoopy's worn-out ears.

'No speaking,' said Sammi. 'You need to complete the activity silently.'

Elle looked up. The band of cloud sitting above the trees now was like a wave, like it might be rolling slowly towards them.

Eventually Ash took their shoulders gently and shuffled the three of them so Elle could link arms with Chrystal. Fred wouldn't do it, and they couldn't tell him to because you were supposed to do the activity silently.

Ash held out his arm, pleading. Come on, man, just do it.

'We can't set off until everyone is in their unbroken circles,' said Sammi. 'Take a moment to think about what each member of your group will need to get through this. What will they need from you? And what will you need from them?' Sammi looked meaningfully at Elle's group.

I won't need anything, Elle thought automatically. From anyone.

Fred sighed loudly and pushed between Elle and Chrystal. Ash took Chrystal's other arm, and at last they had formed their circle.

Fred could feel Elle's taut muscles in her arm, while Chrystal's arm was small and soft, but heavy, weighing on him. Ever since the pandemic started, when someone touched Fred he felt a charge. During lockdown it was all about social distance, touching was so forbidden, that now his senses were alerted when it happened.

They stood in the silence of the forest, tilted their heads right back to see the giant tops of the trees.

'The circle brings protection,' whispered Laila. 'The circle is open, but not broken. It's energy, it's a sacred space. Can you feel the energy running through us?' She closed her eyes.

'Jesus Christ,' muttered Fred. But for a second it made him wince, seeing Laila with her eyes closed like that. So . . . he tried to find the word . . . trusting.

Once the circle activity was over, Johan and Sammi took each of the four groups to a different starting point. 'Remember your first task is to nominate a leader,' Sammi told their group as she led them up a hill. 'Good luck, enjoy the adventure and I'll see you back at school.' She turned and walked off.

'So, we just head this way?' All of a sudden, Elle felt vulnerable, or responsible, or something. She was surprised by her own feelings. Was it because of Chrystal, standing there looking lost already, or Fred with the cans? Johan said that kids loved to be unprotected, unsupervised, to have adventures, and he was giving them the opportunity to do that.

'Yep, head that way, and stay on this track until you reach the first bucket. In about four kilometres. And that's it! Bye!' Sammi gave a wave as she made her way down the hill back to the clearing and the bus.

Four

So off they set, walking along a flat, rough track into the forest.
Elle checked her watch: 3:58. The sun wouldn't go down for
about two hours. Dappled light fell across the path in front
of them, and as they went further in, the trees got even taller,
the trunks of the mountain ashes so straight, so solid. Dark
at the base, in sunshine at the top.

'Look how high they are,' said Ash, craning his neck to
see where they ended in the sky. 'You know they're the tallest
flowering plant in the world?'

'Mountain ash?' said Elle.

Ash nodded, still looking up. 'Those clouds are moving
quickly, check it out.'

The track started up a gradual hill, and Chrystal lagged
behind the others.

'What was with that circle shit?' said Fred.

'It's real,' said Laila. 'You cast the circle so that only positive
energies can enter it. It's like . . . protection.'

'Right . . .' Fred rolled his eyes at Ash.

Ash stayed quiet.

'Did you learn that from your dad?' Fred asked. He felt the black stone in his pocket.

'Partly from him,' said Laila, 'and partly from my own life.'

They stopped and waited for Chrystal to catch up. Laila put her hand on the trunk of a towering tree beside the track. 'Everything in life is a vibration.'

'Didn't Einstein say that?' said Ash before Fred could snigger. They kept walking. 'My dad says it.'

'Don't say anything against the dad,' Fred muttered to Ash, 'I reckon she thinks he's some kind of god.'

After the first hill, they walked along drier slopes where it wasn't too dense or steep. 'This is easy,' said Fred. 'This isn't even a challenge.'

Chrystal was always a few metres behind them. It's going to be really annoying if she walks at this pace the whole time, thought Elle.

On either side of the track were tall eucalypts, blue gums with their smooth bark, messmates. In the gullies, there were wattles and blackwoods. On the forest floor, ferns, grasses and mosses. Ash knew there were so many different types of ferns. Some of the stems were used as medicine by the local Aboriginal people.

'Remember the start of the pandemic,' said Ash, 'when they shut the forest?'

'That's what the government said,' said Laila, 'but people can't shut a forest. It'll keep growing, it'll come to you.' She smiled with her own secret understanding. 'Dad says it beckons you in.'

Fred was suddenly reminded of a painting he'd seen as a child. A girl in the bush, like she'd been beckoned into a forest. Lost. He remembered it because the artist had the same name as him – Frederick.

The afternoon sun shone; the walking was easy. Tiny scrub wrens darted, half skipping, half flying in front of them. They came to a fallen tree across the track, ripped from the soil, some roots exposed and some gripping the earth, reaching down, still living. They leant against it, waiting as Chrystal walked heavily up towards them. 'She's like an annoying little kid who has to tag along,' Fred muttered.

'You know fallen trees are good for the forest?' said Ash, ignoring Fred and taking off his jacket. 'They get absorbed back into the soil. It's a cycle. And see how the sun's shining down here? A fallen tree makes a gap in the canopy, lets the light in.'

'Thanks, Professor.' Fred laughed.

'No problems, any time!' Ash chuckled, squatting to put his jacket into his pack. He stood back up, heard the wind above, saw the tops of the trees swaying against the moving clouds. It made him feel a bit dizzy. He swung his pack over his shoulder. 'Everyone right to keep going?'

Ash was aware that they hadn't elected a leader yet, but he wasn't sure whether he should say something. Sammi had said it was their first task. They should have done it by now.

Laila must have been thinking the same, because after springing effortlessly over the fallen tree, she said, 'Hey, we need to choose our leader.'

'Do you want to be leader?' Elle asked her.

'I think it should be you, Elle,' said Laila.

A pang of disappointment caught Ash by surprise. Why didn't Laila nominate him?

Laila opened her drawstring bag, and took out some smooth purple stones.

Fred smirked.

'Amethyst,' she said, 'for protection on the journey.' Laila took Fred's hand and dropped a stone into it. Fred felt again the touch, her fingers on his palm. Her eyes were green and glistening. Slate Green. He held the stone, then dropped it. Ash bent to pick it up. He handed it to Fred, who smiled and dropped it again.

'Don't be a dick about it, Fred,' Ash said quietly. 'Just take the stone.'

Next, Laila placed a stone in Ash's hand.

'Thanks, Laila. Where do these ones come from?'

'From Dad. He has them for his workshops.'

Elle took her stone politely, thanked Laila. Sometimes Laila went over the top, but she was probably the most relaxed person Elle knew, so there could be something in it, the whole chakra and crystal thing. And there was something soothing about holding a stone in your hand, feeling its energy stored inside. Elle put it in the pocket of her hiking pants, felt it against her hip through the thin material.

Chrystal took her stone, stared at it like a toddler who was wondering if she should put it in her mouth. Then she shoved it in her pocket and kept wringing her hands, looking at the sky.

'Is that the one you're wearing? Amethyst? On the bracelet?' Ash asked Laila.

'No, that's rose quartz.'

'Is that good for travel as well?'

'More for emotional wellbeing,' said Laila. 'It opens the heart chakra.'

'Right,' said Ash. He loved Laila's voice, loved the soft, singsong way she spoke, even if he didn't understand half of what she was on about.

'I'm giving you these for protection. Because when you go into a forest, you leave part of yourself outside it.'

'What part?' asked Fred, almost giggling.

'The part that thinks about everyday life.' Laila spread her arms wide, closed her eyes. 'The stone will help you let the forest in.'

Elle did the same, she tried, but she couldn't help thinking of practical things. Like they should keep going, make some solid progress.

'Would you like to be the leader, Laila?' asked Ash. 'I reckon it should be you. You've given us the stones and stuff.'

Laila opened her eyes, dropped her arms back by her sides. 'I think it should be Elle,' she repeated.

'Fine by me,' said Ash. He would have liked to give it a try, but Elle would be good. She was probably the obvious choice. Elle was his friend, and anyway, he wasn't a jealous person, he wasn't competitive. He pushed the thought away.

'Should it be a guy?' asked Fred.

'Get with the program, mate,' said Ash, 'that's very last century thinking. What do you reckon, Chrystal?' he asked.

'Fine by me,' said Chrystal, too loudly, too brightly, as if she was reciting lines in a play or something, imitating Ash who had said the same thing.

What was fine by her? thought Ash. That Elle was leader? Last century thinking?

He turned to Elle. 'Okay by you?'

'Sure,' said Elle, 'if everyone's down with it.'

No one said anything more, so Elle was leader.

Off they set again. Elle checked the watch: 4:40. 'We're going to basically be up all night,' she said. 'By the time we get back to school and debrief and stuff, we probably won't go to sleep till like three am.'

'I'm already tired,' said Chrystal, walking slowly.

For god's sake, thought Elle, we don't need her moaning for the next eight hours. Elle had to consciously shorten her steps. Walking at a slower pace than was natural was just about the most frustrating thing in the world.

'Didn't you sleep?' Laila asked.

'Mmmmmmmmmmm I can never get to sleep.'

'I can give you a hematite stone if you like.'

Chrystal didn't respond, so Laila went on. 'Before you go to bed, you hold it, close your eyes and visualise having a good night's sleep. Then put it under your pillow.'

Like a ritual, thought Elle. 'So the healing stones are a kind of art?' she asked Laila.

'You can look at it like that.'

They kept walking. 'My dad is a bit like an artist,' said Laila after a minute.

'Yeah,' muttered Fred, 'a bullshit artist.'

Ash wasn't sure if Laila had heard Fred. She seemed to ignore him, walking a little ahead with Elle. 'You don't know him,' said Ash, 'you've never met him.'

They walked on. No one spoke for a while. Elle glanced up at the soaring gums. She could hear birds but she couldn't see them.

'I reckon mountain ash would have to be my favourite tree,' she said. 'You know they can grow to a hundred metres tall?'

Instinctively, they all looked up. Long ribbons of bark hung from the canopy above, swaying in the breeze up there. Down on the track, the air was still and quiet, except for the tiny twittering of the scrub wrens and robins.

Fred remembered another one. Mineral Green. And the grey trunks. Sleek.

But, 'Forget trees,' he said, because Elle had given him an idea. 'Favourite band?'

Everyone got into the game.

'Can it be a solo artist or does it have to be a band?'

'Favourite colour?'

'Favourite colour's boring,' said Fred. 'I know, favourite food, favourite death-row meal!'

'Is that even a thing?' Elle asked.

'Yeah, you can Google it, find out what different criminals ordered. Like the Oklahoma bomber, for his last meal he got a kilo of mint choc-chip ice-cream.' Fred shook his head. 'Like a little kid. And one guy wanted an olive. What sort of idiot would order one olive? When you could have anything you want!'

'You wouldn't need to worry about calories,' said Elle.

'Most people order stuff like fried chicken,' Fred said. 'Shrimp. Hey, Chrystal, is that a thing in America? They all wanted fried shrimp. Is that like prawns, here?'

No response.

'Comfort food,' said Elle. 'I wonder if you can have as much as you like. I think I'd choose a burger with the lot. A gourmet one. And a caramel milkshake with extra ice-cream.'

'I'd choose sushi,' said Laila. 'And matcha ice-cream. What about you, Ash?'

Ash found it hard to say his favourite anything. He liked a lot of things, but never felt inclined to say a preference. It was easier to ask other people. 'Favourite book when you were little?' he asked.

'We read fairy tales,' said Laila.

'Have to be *Where the Wild Things Are*,' said Fred.

Elle thought of the books she'd read when she was a kid. Stories of girls riding ponies in the English countryside. Hedges, woodlands, copse and bluebells. Here, it was just bush. Not romantic, but tough. The bush.

They came across a pool. The water looked black. 'It's the tannin from the bark in trees further up the forest,' said Ash. 'See up there, where the creek flows in?' Standing on a rock, he watched their silhouettes reflected on the still water; he and Elle were both taller than Fred. It reminded him of another of Sammi's team-building activities where you had to arrange a group of people from tallest to shortest without speaking. It would have made a good photo, their silhouettes all lined up like a chain of paper cut-outs – but they didn't have their phones, and anyway the wind blew, the light changed and they all disappeared in the ripples. Ash heard whooshing above, and the close sound of their steps on the stony track as they walked on.

Elle and Laila led the way again, followed by Ash and Fred, and Chrystal just behind them. They stopped at the top of a rise to wait for her. They all had proper walking shoes, tough underneath on the rocky path that was the colour of clay. But Chrystal's runners were those really light ones. They were going to get wet. Or she'd roll her ankle or something. Chrystal wouldn't cope with that, thought Elle. She had no resilience.

Elle was frustrated with all this waiting already, but Laila was kind.

'I know, I'll give you the black tourmaline, it'll help,' she said.

It's only because Laila hasn't had to put up with her non-stop for the past three weeks, Elle thought crossly.

Laila rummaged in her drawstring bag. 'It's not here.' She looked again. 'Did I leave it in the main hall? When we were doing yoga.'

'You must have,' said Elle, 'if it's not in the bag. Doesn't matter. Come on, let's keep going. We'll get to the first bucket soon.' They'd done the timing in the prep classes. Four ks would take about an hour, depending on the terrain. They could probably do five ks in an hour if the track was easy. The creek was far below, it made a gentle tumbling sound.

Laila frowned. 'I hope I haven't lost it.'

'I bet it's back at school,' said Ash. 'I'm sure you'll find it.'

Laila didn't seem to be listening to him. 'It's a very powerful stone. It gives protection,' she said, looking to the treetops being blown around.

'Hey, look!' Fred picked up a stone from the path, held it out. 'I found it!'

'Very funny,' said Laila, putting the bag back in her backpack.

'Probably works just as well,' he said, hurling the stone away.

He was such a smartarse! 'Honestly,' said Elle, 'Laila does yoga, she's got some gemstones – why does it bother you so much? You don't have to like them, but what gives you the right to stop her from believing in whatever she believes in?'

'Woah, this leader thing is going to your head already,' said Fred. 'I was just mucking around.'

No one spoke, and they walked on.

Fred hated the way he was nasty like this. What did he care about the gemstones? Why had he taken that black one, back at school? Still, he kept baiting people, being a stirrer, like it was some weird pain relief. He kicked out at a rock on the path. 'Laila knows I was joking, don't you, Laila?'

'Yeah,' said Laila, 'don't worry, it's all good.'

Fred watched her as they walked, in single file now, along the rough path. She took even steps. Laila's mind seemed so quiet, undisturbed, whereas his was filled with commotion. Fred was smart, teachers had told him that, but he couldn't harness his smartness like other people could. He did and said things without thinking. And if he really did think, like now, he knew he didn't want to offend Laila, to hurt her feelings, he actually liked her even though she was a total woo-woo hippie. But he couldn't stop.

The hill was getting steeper. 'It's a bit of a climb,' Ash puffed.

Fred overtook him, running, his pack banging against his back. 'Not for me!' He gave Ash a shove as he passed.

'Fred!' said Elle, 'watch it!' They couldn't have Fred bagging people for the next eight hours, it wasn't fair. And Elle was the leader, she was allowed to pull him up on stuff. When it was necessary. In class, they'd talked about leadership, about how different leaders around the world had dealt with the pandemic. Elle thought Jacinda Ardern was the best. She remembered the three things they'd discussed – empathy, direction, meaning. And demonstrating resilience. Elle was good at relying solely on herself – going to lots of schools and living in different parts of the world had taught her that. So being a leader shouldn't be difficult. And there were only five of them, including Elle – Jacinda Ardern had a whole country to lead! Think of it as an adventure, Elle told herself. It doesn't matter if Fred's a pain, if Chrystal is difficult, she'll be gone soon, back to Madison, Wisconsin, and, as her dad had asked, Elle would make an effort. She smiled across at Chrystal. 'How are you going?'

No answer.

'This looks like one of the old logging tracks,' said Ash as the path widened. 'I could tell you a bit about the area, Chrystal, if you like.' Sure, he wasn't the leader, but he could still contribute.

'Chrystal? If you're interested? This whole area was logged for railway sleepers, like two hundred years ago.'

Chrystal said nothing.

'Chryst—'

'I'm not interested.'

That was a pity, because Ash did know quite a lot about the forest, the landscape, the environment they were moving through. Come to think of it, he probably knew more than Elle. Disappointment nagged at him again, but you can't get everything you want. He wasn't that type of person. He was generous, fair, a team player.

The track was flat again for a while, wider and less rocky, so they could walk in pairs. The ground beneath them had give, from the damp earth. Gum leaves formed a leathery carpet of pink, red, grey, brown, along with strips of bark and tree roots.

Elle and Laila led the way, then Chrystal in the middle, and Ash and Fred at the back.

Laila was quiet.

'Everything okay?' Elle asked her.

'Do you think Joe would have taken that stone? He was in the hall at lunchtime.' Laila looked down at the track. 'I thought he was going to do yoga, like he used to.'

'I don't reckon he would have taken it,' said Elle. Joe was the only person who seemed to stress Laila. They'd had a bad break-up. He'd really hurt her. It was last year that all that happened, when half the time they weren't at school, and the only person Laila saw was Joe. She still seemed kind of connected to him, aware if he was ever nearby.

'Hey, how long have we been walking for?' Fred called.

Elle checked the watch. 'An hour. It's 5:04. We must be nearly at the bucket. It shouldn't take us more than an hour to walk four ks.'

'Most of it's been uphill, though,' said Ash.

'Yeah it's pretty steep,' added Fred. 'Be good when we're going downhill.'

From behind, Fred noticed again that Chrystal had an odd gait; clumsy and unco. She kept her head down and one leg went out to the side a bit below the knee. Laila was the opposite, she almost floated, each step the same length, hardly touching the ground, like one of those gazelles in nature documentaries.

Effortless. But Chrystal, it looked as if she was using up too much energy – physical, mental, something like that.

She sighed. She was always sighing.

'What's with the stuffed toy?' Fred called out to Chrystal.

Great, thought Elle. He's finished with Laila and now he starts on Chrystal.

Chrystal stopped. 'It's Snoopy.' She shoved Snoopy in Fred's face. 'Want to meet him?'

'Weirdo,' said Fred under his breath, glancing at Ash, hoping he would agree. Didn't this chick care that people would laugh at her? But it looked as if she needed the toy more than she cared about the laughter. She even spoke to it like it was alive.

'She's got a toy,' said Ash. 'Just leave it, mate. Who cares. Come on, keep going or we'll never get there.' Then to Chrystal, to the group, he said, 'Did you ever read the *Peanuts* comics? With Snoopy in them? I really liked them when I was a kid. Wasn't there a TV show? A movie?'

'They were supposed to be called *Li'l folks*,' said Chrystal. 'Not *Peanuts*.'

'Right,' said Ash, relieved that he'd lessened the tension a bit. 'I used to wonder what the peanuts meant. I always liked Linus,' he continued after a minute.

'Lucy was funny,' said Fred.

Humming, humming, then, 'Charlie Brown isn't bald,' said Chrystal. 'He has light hair, cut short so you can't see it.'

'Oh, right, okay. And –'

'Charlie Brown's father is a barber. His mother is a house-wife.' She paused. 'You never see the adults.'

Ash laughed. 'Hey, Chrystal, if you were on *Hard Quiz*, your expert subject could be the *Peanuts* comics.'

Elle felt relieved that Fred had stopped being so negative and aggressive to everyone. She hardly knew him, but already she sensed he could be difficult. She wanted to ask him for the torches and phone, because she was the leader now, but something in her sensed that he needed to feel important too, that this was the way she'd need to work with him, so she said nothing. It doesn't matter who carries them, she reassured herself.

'Hey, you're right, Chrystal, there aren't any adults in those comics!' Ash was saying. 'I'd never realised that.' Like us now, he thought. He marched alongside Fred. The mood was better. Lighter. Ash felt strong, like he could walk through this forest easily, into the night and out again. He'd got everyone back on an even keel, bringing up the *Peanuts* thing. They hadn't gone far into the forest, but already he felt brave and glad they were just five kids on their own. 'There's something great about being in charge of ourselves,' he said. 'Don't you reckon?'

61

Five

They each fell into their own rhythm. Elle and Ash were the fastest, so they set the speed. They got used to stopping every few minutes and waiting for Chrystal. Elle knew from doing cross-country that it was important for your stamina to go at your own pace. But Chrystal was SO slow!

Although the sun was low in the sky now, they'd warmed up. Elle took off her hoodie. Ash was wearing only a t-shirt under his high-vis. Easter time was like that, unpredictable weather. Sometimes Easter can be like a summer holiday; everyone at the beach and the lifesaver flags flying brightly in the sun. Sometimes it can feel like winter already; still, cold air, all the wood heaters going and smoke sitting in the valley.

The trees here were so tall. Big sheets of bark peeled back from the massive trunks like an old skin, showing the smooth new colours underneath. Other bark pieces hung, caught on a branch or a fork in a tree, like giant mobiles. The young branches at the top swayed in slow motion. It reminded Ash of kelp swirling in the sea. And beyond the trees, high in the sky, a flock of small birds shone, tiny slivers of silver turning in the sunlight against the grey clouds behind. They didn't look like coastal birds to Ash, which made him wonder if they were deeper into the forest than they realised.

Okay, this is better, thought Elle. The sun's going down, but it's still light. And it's not all uphill anymore. Now I need to make an effort with Fred. Just talk naturally to him.

'So, you were at Bellarine Grammar before OCS?' she asked.

Fred nodded.

'Do you know Maisie Liu? She was there last year, I think.'

'Don't think so.'

'She was at the international school in Hong Kong with me. We still message each other.'

'I was only there for two terms. I didn't meet many boarders from overseas, didn't really hang out with the international school kids. They're so OTT,' Fred said.

Was he having a go at her, now? But Elle did kind of get what Fred meant. She'd noticed at OCS that kids seemed a bit more relaxed, they didn't have to perform, put their best foot forward, get noticed. Girls weren't so competitive with each other. Of course, there were all kinds of kids at international schools, just like any other school. But there was that upfront nature to many of them. Elle had learnt that she had to connect quickly, get her personality across, fast-track friendships because who knew for how long any of them would be there before their parents took them and moved on to some other city, country, region of the world. Part of you really wanted to make friends, and part of you knew that it'd be temporary. Did it make friendships more intense? Maybe.

'Do you have kids from different places at your school?' Elle asked Chrystal. 'International students? In Madison?'

'Wisconsin,' said Chrystal.

'Yeah, Madison, in Wisconsin,' said Elle.

Chrystal didn't answer the question – couldn't, wouldn't, as usual Elle wasn't sure.

'Can you walk a bit faster?' said Fred. 'To match the rest of us? Come on, Chrystal, you're holding us up. And you can take your sunglasses off. It's not sunny anymore.'

Elle knew there was no point getting exasperated with her. Even though Chrystal was difficult, Elle got the feeling she wasn't trying to be that way. Recently, there had been moments, usually when other people were annoyed or baffled by Chrystal, when Elle felt a bit sorry for her, almost as if she had to protect her, mother her.

They were in a valley now, the ferns were taller, and the mountain ash, too. They clambered over another fallen tree.

'Bloody trees everywhere,' said Fred.

'Fred,' laughed Ash, 'it's a forest!' Different for everyone, he thought. A tree to Laila was something spiritual, to hold her body against, feel its timeless energy. To Fred, it was something in the way. A big immoveable something.

Laila halted halfway across the fallen tree. A butterfly, grey, black and indigo blue, had landed on her hand. Laila was always touching things: the trees, the stones, the fronds of a fern. She even held her own arms when she stood still. And you always knew when Laila was near because she put her hand on your shoulder, or your arm. They had laughed last year with the social distancing rules. How had Laila coped!

'You know the caterpillar doesn't actually turn into a butterfly in its cocoon?' said Ash.

Fred laughed. 'What! You mean *The Very Hungry Caterpillar* lied to us all? Didn't it change into a butterfly after eating all that stuff?' Fred could picture the bold colours. The watermelon, the apple, the yellow wedge of cheese.

'It doesn't transform, it decomposes, falls apart completely, literally dies.' Ash looked closely at the blue wings, like petals, on Laila's hand. 'That poor butterfly had to put itself together, from scratch.'

'It did a beautiful job,' said Laila, holding her hand still, the blue so intense in the dusky, even light of the forest.

'Yeah,' said Ash quietly, watching as the butterfly took off, fluttering its velvety wings.

'Come on,' said Elle, 'we can't keep stopping every five minutes for a science lesson, we'll never get anywhere.' She smiled, and Ash did too. He could take a joke.

•

They reached the first bucket at 5:17, according to Elle's dad's watch. It was a new bucket, red like Johan had told them, sitting bright and clean at the edge of the track. Fred ran ahead to it.

'So we did four ks in just over an hour,' said Elle, calculating in her head as she spoke. 'I s'pose that's not bad, because we stopped a bit. But we should probably pick up the pace.'

Fred had taken the note from inside the bucket, and he read aloud: 'Continue on for five kilometres, until you reach a fork in the path.'

'This is easy.' Fred screwed up the note and dropped it back in the bucket. 'This'll take us like an hour, tops. We don't even need the compass! Or a leader! Who's been to all the international schools, lived all over the world.'

'We might need it later,' said Elle, ignoring Fred's sarcasm. 'The compass. It might be one of those orienteering things that starts off easy and gets more difficult.' The compass was in Fred's bag, with the torches and the phone, and the Double Blacks.

Fred lifted his pack. 'Anyway, it's good we haven't got any teachers with us,' he was saying to Ash, 'telling us what to do. Watching us.'

'Hey, what did you do with the note?' said Elle. 'We should keep them.'

Fred picked the screwed-up piece of paper from the bucket and threw it at Elle, not so she'd catch it, but so it would hit her. But she did catch it, quickly, one-handed. She flattened it out against her thigh, folded it, and put it in the pocket of her pants with the stone.

They went on, the path widened out, some of the trees were blackened. 'Must have been a fire,' said Ash. 'A controlled burn.' The dead stumps looked like tombstones.

'Yeah . . .' Elle was preoccupied. She was worried about the stuff Fred had in his bag. She knew it would cause problems. She had to take responsibility. Leaders sometimes had to make unpopular decisions. 'Hang on, guys,' she said as they reached a bend in the track. Ash stopped. 'Just wait for a sec.'

Fred stopped, too. Light was falling.

'As leader, I'm asking you to ditch the alcohol, Fred. I'd feel more comfortable, I think we all would, if you left it here.'

'No way, it cost me money.'

'Let's have a vote.'

Fred groaned, dumped his pack.

'We're not supposed to bring anything like that with us.'

I'd feel more comfortable . . . God, she sounded like Fred's lame stepdad, Marcus. Mr I'm Just Trying To Be Reasonable. Mr We Don't Feel Comfortable.

'Raise your hand if you think we should leave the alcohol here,' said Elle.

No one moved. Trees creaked overhead. A thin branch tumbled to the ground.

Laila put up her hand.

Then Ash.

'Chrystal?'

Fred and Chrystal exchanged a look.

'I vote keep it,' said Chrystal, looking past them all, rubbing Snoopy's ears.

She just did that to annoy me, thought Elle.

Then Elle had an idea.

'Okay, you can keep one can. That's a compromise.'

'Oh great,' said Fred sarcastically, 'thanks, boss. Some party it'll be with one bloody can.'

He pulled out one can of Double Black and dropped the plastic bag with the rest of them on the ground by the track.

'Can you please put it by that stump? The burnt one? If you really want it back, you can ask Johan where we started and come and get it tomorrow. We're just past where we found the first bucket, not that far from the starting point.' Surely that was reasonable?

'Now we have to litter, leave rubbish,' said Ash. 'I hate doing that.'

'It's not rubbish,' said Fred grumpily. 'It's my stash.'

Fred dropped it down beside the blackened tree stump, did up his pack again, and they walked on.

No one spoke for a while. Chrystal's low humming was like a continuous soundtrack. It sounded to Ash like the beginning of a song by some strange new band, as if other instruments might start up any minute. Everyone played an instrument at OCS. Elle did piano. Ash guitar. Laila played the double bass. A big, ungainly instrument, but Ash had watched her play it, her long fingers moving and pressing evenly against the thick strings, holding it against her body as if it was part of her, her head slightly tilted towards it. Ash knew that feeling of music vibrating through you, from the way he held his guitar. Fred would have to choose an instrument soon. Maybe drums? It was the only thing Ash could imagine him playing. He looked across at Fred, head down, frowning, marching up the hill. Ash wasn't sure whether Fred would fit in at OCS. It didn't sound like he'd fitted in at Bellarine Grammar, and Ash couldn't imagine Fred at the local high school either, with the kids who'd lived in the area all their lives, whose parents were farmers, or worked in the timber mill, the ice-cream factory, or the abattoir.

The track narrowed again, they were heading uphill. Elle led the way. In front of them, the band of cloud was lower, and the fluffy clouds weren't white anymore, parts of them were dark grey. And now there was an eerie light, a strange brightness, like a retro Instagram filter, all around them. It reminded Elle of being in the tropics. That yellow light before a downpour, that made her think of palm trees and coconuts, not mountain ash and ferns.

She checked the time: 5:43. She could still see it without pressing the light.

Fred overtook Elle. Now Laila and Ash were walking together, Fred was in front and Elle and Chrystal in the middle.

'How's your headache?' Elle asked Chrystal.

'I still have it.'

'Did you take the Panadol?'

Chrystal stopped. 'It's because a storm is coming.'

'Chrystal, they told us, the weather isn't supposed to change until –'

But Chrystal wasn't listening. 'I can feel it.'

'– until tomorrow morning,' Elle continued. 'Just a bit of rain tonight. Remember, Johan said? And after that, it's only a chance of thunderstorms.'

Ash slowed down.

'Ash, we can't keep stopping,' said Elle.

He turned to them. 'You know that's a thing? When there's a decrease in atmospheric pressure, it makes a difference between the outside air and the air in your sinuses. That's what causes pain, like a headache.'

Chrystal's humming got louder. 'I get tinnitus, too. When the weather's going to change.'

'Do you have that now?' asked Ash.

Chrystal nodded again, twisting poor Snoopy in a knot.

'Listen, it's nothing to worry about. Johan told us that!' Elle was getting impatient. 'He would have looked at the app,' she added. Although she had to admit, that yellow-grey light was stressing her a bit. 'Come on, keep up.'

'Knowing Johan though,' Ash said, 'he'd make us do this no matter what the weather forecast is. They reckon he didn't even want us to have one phone.'

'Yeah, some of the parents say he really pushes the envelope,' said Laila.

Chrystal looked puzzled.

'What envelope?'

•

They followed the track as it continued uphill, the sun going down now behind them. Even after sunset there would still be some light in the sky. Particularly this yellow-grey cloud.

'It's pretty steep, isn't it.' Ash puffed beside Laila.

She didn't puff at all, just glided up the hill. When they got to the top, Laila turned to him and smiled. She gave off such a calming energy. Ash liked to be around her.

The others caught up, at the top of a ridge now, and the five of them stood, looking out over the landscape. Huge swathes of the last rays of sunlight cut through the clouds and across the valley. Everything was green and golden. The grasses in the foreground waved in the light, gum leaves glistened beyond them, and the hills disappeared on the misty horizon.

'Wow, look at that,' said Ash.

No one spoke. Ash could see where the forest had been chopped off, ended, and farmland began. Once it had all been forest, right down to the ocean. Imagine clearing it, he thought. He sensed that Laila, beside him, was still, and breathing deeply, in the presence of something, connecting. She'd pulled up the sleeves of her mohair jumper, and the sleeves of her loose cotton top had come up too. Laila's arms were long and smooth, the rose quartz bracelet falling against her wrist. Her eyes were closed, as if she was somewhere else. Her eyelashes were very black.

Even Fred was quiet for a moment. Then he broke the spell. 'How long have we been walking for?' He turned away from the view. 'This is pretty boring.'

Elle checked the watch. 'Fred, we're not even two hours in. We'll be hiking for eight hours. Didn't you do hiking at Bellarine? Don't they have that campus in a forest?'

'That's for Year Ten.' Fred pushed past Elle to be at the front again. 'I just did the surfing camps.'

Anyway, what's the point of hiking? Fred thought. Why make yourself more uncomfortable than you already were.

'We did a hike in Year Eight,' he remembered. 'Each group had a number, and when we got to the summit we had to tear that page number out of an old book and bring it back. As proof that we'd made it.'

'That's a good idea,' said Ash. 'Did you get there?'

Fred chuckled. 'We got someone else to get our page. Tricked them. It was so funny.'

No one responded. 'Yeah, it was really funny,' Fred went on, filling the silence.

'Funny,' echoed Chrystal in her monotone from behind them.

'The Year Sevens and Eights did heaps of cool stuff. Like there was this thing called Sleeping Beauties. Have you guys ever done that?'

'Never heard of it,' said Elle.

'You have to take photos of people sleeping. Like a dare. When people are asleep they look like little kids.' Fred laughed, but he felt hot, he wanted to shut up but couldn't. 'Even adults.'

'What, you took photos of people when they were sleeping?' asked Elle.

'Not me –' began Fred.

'I think that's a bit creepy.'

'Heaps of boarders did it. It was a craze. At other schools, too. Like, pranking.' Who was he trying to impress, here? 'I thought you'd know it.'

'Well we don't,' Elle snapped.

She looked to the sky, which was fading now to a deep blue. Night was coming. Two black cockatoos, yellow tails, flew slowly above them. 'See the way they move in slow motion,' said Laila quietly, almost sadly. Elle knew that when Laila had broken up with Joe, he had photos of her, too – photos that he'd asked her to take, and that he had taken. Laila had never shown them to Elle, but she'd told her about them, and she worried what he might do with them now that they'd broken up. Elle watched the cockatoos cruise effortlessly, rising a little with each long, even wingbeat. 'If they're near the coast,' Laila went on, 'it means rain.'

Chrystal stopped. 'Is that a fact? Is that true?' She turned to Ash.

Ash shrugged. 'I don't know.' Ash knew a bit, but really, he hardly knew anything. Not like his friends in the Kimberley, who could read the bush, not even read it, just be in it and understand all its rhythms and signs. 'I think birds do come down to the lower branches before bad weather,' he said. 'I heard that somewhere, but I'm no expert.'

Chrystal looked up, gripping Snoopy. 'See how high in the sky they are,' Ash continued, trying to reassure her. 'If a big rain was coming they'd be flying lower down. They avoid air pressure changes by flying low.'

'Jesus, mate,' Fred laughed, 'you're a walking encyclopedia.'

'I'm not,' said Ash. He didn't want to be a fraud, come across as some kind of expert when he wasn't. He watched the cockatoos. They were kind of hypnotising. Such graceful flyers, their wings flapped in a heavy, fluid rhythm.

As if the cockatoos could see them down on the ground, they let out a loud, wailing call that carried through the valley. In the dying light it was a spooky sound.

I'm glad we've got torches, Ash thought, knowing that in an hour or so they'd be hiking in the dark.

'What about snakes?' said Chrystal suddenly.

'It's too cold for –' began Ash.

'Look out!' yelled Fred. 'There's one now!'

Chrystal froze.

Fred laughed. 'Even I know snakes don't come out at night, Chrystal.'

Now Chrystal was going even more slowly, as if every tree root was a snake. Great, thought Elle. Thanks, Fred.

Ash tried to calm her down, take her mind off the non-existent snakes.

'What are the forests like in Wisconsin?'

'There are deer,' said Chrystal after a pause. 'And the trees are different. Our trees lose their leaves in fall.'

'We have trees like that, too,' began Ash, but Chrystal kept going – 'Willow, ash, cedar, oak,' reeling them off as if she'd learnt them as a child, like the times tables.

'But they're not native to Australia,' said Ash, 'so you don't see them in forests like this. We have beech trees, but ours in Victoria don't lose their leaves. Australia has hardly any deciduous native trees,' he added. 'I know there's a beech in Tasmania that's deciduous, though. Like ash trees.' He smiled. 'Golden ash, claret ash, they lose their leaves in autumn. Fall,' he added so it would make sense to Chrystal. 'And we have deer, too.' He fell back, walking beside her now. 'Did you have to learn about Australia before you came here?'

No response.

'Did you get to choose where you wanted to go?'

Then, just when you thought she was never going to answer, she did.

'Australians are laidback, friendly people. They have a –' Chrystal put her hands up, making the quote marks, '– "fair-go" attitude.'

Something else she'd learnt by rote.

'Yeah, I don't know how true that is,' said Ash. 'It's a pretty big generalisation. Australians can be racist . . .' He paused.

'And mean,' said Fred.

'And sometimes homophobic . . .' added Ash.

Chrystal said nothing.

'How about in America though? With the riots. Did they have Black Lives Matter rallies in Madison?'

Chrystal didn't seem to want to talk about any of it. Or anything. At all.

Elle was grateful to Ash for trying. She really liked that about him. So often, girls had to ask all the questions and guys just talked about themselves.

'Poor Ash, Chrystal's so hard to talk to,' Elle said quietly to Laila. 'I'm sure she's on the spectrum, or something.'

'Yeah, she's vibrating at a different frequency,' said Laila, walking lightly over the uneven path.

•

The day was gradually fading. Birds called in the evening air. Rosellas, the screech of a cockatoo, another call that sounded like flute music.

'It must be nearly five ks,' said Elle. 'We've gone faster because it hasn't all been uphill. Look out for a fork in the track.'

The forest opened up again and they could see areas that had been logged. Broken trunks, splintered, wrecked trees, fallen branches, like a forest graveyard.

'Hasn't the government said they'll protect old growth forest?' said Ash.

'Yeah they have, but it's complicated in how you define "old growth". It's not as straightforward as it sounds.' Elle had heard her mum and dad discussing it.

They came to a rotting wooden sign with worn-out lettering that no one could read. 'I reckon it's the name of the creek,' said Ash. There was a narrow creek, more like a trickle, a miniature waterfall, with a rock-crossing to what looked like an old four-wheel-drive track heading along the top of the hill. 'I think the teachers said there'd be a creek crossing.'

'I found it!'

'Go, Fred!'

Behind the sign was the second bucket. In the dim light the red was still clear, and the number 2 was painted on with that reflector paint that would be easy to see if you shone a torch.

There were two tracks now, the walking track they'd been on, and the one that crossed the creek and went up the hill. A fork in the path.

Fred took the paper from under a rock in the bucket and angled it to the last of the light. 'Walk north to the top of the next ridge,' he read. 'So, this track.' He pointed, and took off.

'Hang on, Fred,' said Elle, 'can you give me the note? We better check the compass and the map. This creek's a good landmark. And does anyone else want some water?' she asked. They'd been walking for two hours now, uphill for a lot of it. Elle remembered that they were supposed to take a short break, like for ten minutes, at every bucket. At bucket five they'd be halfway, and could stop for a bit longer and eat their sandwiches, have a warm drink. Elle checked the watch, pressed the light: 6:03. They were still doing well with the time. They should reach a bucket approximately every fifty minutes, that's what Johan had said.

Everyone drank from their water bottles, except Fred, who went over to the creek crossing, squatted and held his hands under the trickle of water. 'We're not supposed to drink the creek water,' Elle called. 'We've got heaps of water here. I've got a spare –' Fred immediately cupped the water to his mouth.

'What did you do that for?'

Chrystal copied him.

'Chrystal, don't do that.' Sometimes it seemed as if Chrystal was much younger than the rest of them. She wanted Fred to like her, but he was never going to like her, they all knew that, she was too weird.

Chrystal shuffled over to them, water marks on her grey runners already.

'We need to check the compass,' said Elle, 'make sure we're walking north. May as well hand out the torches, too, before it gets too dark. 'Fred?' she called. 'Can you stop? Can you bring your bag?'

But Fred was heading up the hill.

'Fred, stop!'

He slowed down, and they ran up to reach him. Higher on the slope, the breeze really picked up, and from somewhere way down below they could hear the ocean. Or was that wind?

'Can you get out the torches?' Elle asked, putting her hoodie back on.

Fred opened his backpack. The one can lay on top of his spray jacket, like a reminder of a bad time. He rummaged through the pack.

'Hang on . . .'

He looked up at the group. 'Did I have them?'

'Yeah,' said Elle, 'you put them in your backpack when Johan handed them out. With the phone they gave us, and the map.'

Fred stood up.

'What?'

'Oh shit.'

'What?'

'They were in the plastic bag. With the cans.'

'So they're back by the track where we left the cans?'

Fred looked through the backpack again, but it was useless. He had put them on top, in the plastic bag, and now they were an hour back through the forest.

'If you hadn't made me get rid of them, this wouldn't have happened.'

'It's not Elle's fault,' said Laila evenly.

'Well it's not mine!' said Fred.

Elle knew this was a pointless conversation. And Ash wasn't saying anything. 'Did anyone else bring a torch?' she asked.

'They told us not to, remember,' said Laila. 'Johan said they'd provide one for each person and that was all we were allowed.'

'And we need the compass,' added Ash.

'If we keep going quickly we won't need a torch anyway,' said Fred. 'Which bucket are we up to? The third? I reckon if we walk fast we'll get back before it's totally dark. I reckon the school's just over that hill.'

'Why do you reckon that?' Elle asked. 'We're only at the second bucket. They said we'd be walking for eight hours, Fred. How can school be just over the hill?'

'I reckon it is.'

Elle didn't get it. People just believed their own bullshit these days, no matter what the facts were, what the teachers said, what the experts knew.

'The school's not on the other side of that hill,' said Laila. 'We would have seen it from back there, when we could see over the whole valley. I think we're past Aire's Hill, on the ridge on the other side. If that's right, then we're twenty ks from school.'

Elle nodded. 'And we're not going to get far without a torch or a compass once it gets dark.'

She knew what she had to say next. She was the leader.

'Do you want me to go back and get them?'

Silence.

'Fred should do it,' said Laila. 'That would be fair.'

Fred said nothing, looked at the ground. Then, 'I'm not going all the way back there.'

'Come on, mate, it's your responsibility,' began Ash. 'We need to take responsibility for –'

'Shut up, Ash! You sound like someone's parents.'

Ash was surprised at the way Fred was talking. 'Calm down, mate . . .'

But Fred looked more tense, more uptight. His face, his features were screwed up. He had a small face, small nose and ears. Like a pixie.

'I'll do it,' said Elle. She didn't need the guys to start fighting now. And they were losing light, wasting time. She knew she'd be the fastest runner. And shouldn't a leader make sacrifices for her group? Anyway, she didn't trust Fred. He might take the compass, torches and his cans and go somewhere on his own to drink them.

'You guys wait here. If I run, I'll be back in about an hour.'

'It'll be pitch dark by then,' said Ash.

'I can use a torch on my way back,' said Elle, taking off her high-vis vest.

'Is that rain?'

Elle stopped. 'What?'

'I think I felt a drop.' Ash held out his upturned hand. 'Of rain.'

'Rain?' Chrystal hadn't said a word this whole time. She was standing on her own up the track a bit.

'You okay?' Elle called.

'The storm,' Chrystal said, pulling at her hair. 'There's a storm.'

'There's no storm. For god's sake, Chrystal, can you forget about it?' Elle took off her hoodie again, then put the high-vis back on over her t-shirt, knowing she'd warm up quickly. She dumped her pack on the ground. 'See you guys soon.' She started off at a jog back down the track.

'Be careful,' called Laila, 'mind your step in the dark.'

They watched as Elle's high-vis moved in and out of the trees, until they couldn't see her anymore.

Six

The four of them waited, sitting at the fork in the path. The ground was cold, but the spitting rain had stopped. Still, now that they weren't moving, they noticed that the air was colder, too. The clouds were grey in the darkening sky.

Chrystal was twisting her hair with her fingers. She must pull half of it out, thought Fred. He sat on a clay-coloured rock. 'Someone's been here,' he said, 'someone's spilt paint.' There were white splatters on the rocks and leaves.

'That's not paint,' said Ash, 'it's owl poo. They call it whitewash.'

Fred got out the can. Opened it with a hiss.

'Good on you,' Ash muttered sarcastically into the hood of his jacket. Did he have to do that now?

Fred took a deep, long mouthful, then looked over at Ash, almost willing him to say something more, but no one said anything. There was only the sounds of the forest. Evening sounds. Frogs by the creek somewhere. Birds calling. A kooka-burra, far off.

Ash sat beside Chrystal on a fallen log and got out an apple. 'Does anyone want one?' he asked. 'I've got so much food here.' He shoved a paper bag back in his pack. 'Jamie thinks I'm going to starve.'

'No thanks,' said Laila, sitting against a tree.

Fred skolled more from the can.

'Why does he think you'll starve?' Chrystal pulled at Snoopy's ears. 'Are you going to starve?'

'Don't worry, Chrystal' said Ash, 'it was a joke.'

Fred laughed, nastily. 'Jamie's not a guy, Chrystal. Jamie's female.'

Chrystal looked blank.

'Yep, you got it, Fred.' Ash knew that Fred knew, because he'd been to Ash's place to pick him up with some other guys when they'd been surfing a couple of times. But Ash had never discussed it openly with him. Ash didn't have to talk about it to everyone. It didn't totally define him.

'Jamie is Ash's mum,' said Laila.

'One of them,' Fred smirked. 'He lives with his –'

Ash nodded. 'Mums.'

Fred smiled, slowly. 'Yeah, his mum's a dyke.'

'Shut up, Fred,' said Laila quietly.

It had been a while since someone had spoken to Ash like this, he wasn't used to being on the alert. It never bothered his friends when he lived up north, and from how Ash saw it, they all seemed to have lots of adults around them who were like their parents. Other people were curious, some seemed almost envious, as if he'd be able to get away with anything. Laila

82

knew, his friends at school all knew, they had other friends with same-sex parents.

But it felt as if Fred wanted an argument, wanted to upset Ash, or Laila, or Chrystal, or someone. He hadn't seemed interested in it before, why make a big deal of it now?

'What Fred is saying, Chrystal, is that my mums are in a same-sex relationship,' said Ash calmly. 'Eloise is my mum, and Jamie's my other mum.'

'Woah,' said Fred, 'two mothers. Cool.'

'It's not really cool or not cool. It just is.' Ash was over Fred's sniggering tone.

'You must have a dad as well, then.'

Ash nodded, picking up a stone and throwing it towards the creek. 'He's a friend, he's Paul, I don't call him Dad.'

'So, not a real dad. You don't have a real dad.'

Laila spoke up. 'Everyone's actually okay with this now, Fred. Like the whole world. Even old people are okay with it. So what is your problem?'

Fred felt a rush of anger. Ash had two mothers, and Fred didn't really have one. Not one who cared anymore, anyway. And Fred's mum had Marcus. Fred hated Marcus. Or maybe it was Marcus who hated Fred. It was like his original mother disappeared, died almost, and this new one wasn't interested in him anymore. There was nothing left about him that she enjoyed. And his dad lived in an apartment now, a penthouse, with Louise and her two kids, and she didn't want a teenage boy hanging around. Where did Fred fit in all of this? Nowhere, that's where. He drank again. Held the can there till it was nearly empty, gulped it, felt the bittersweet liquid, the tang of citrus, slide down his throat. 'What makes you think I've got a problem with it?'

'You're being quite hostile,' said Laila in her smooth, soothing voice. 'I'm feeling a negative energy.'

Fred wiped his mouth. This girl was ridiculous.

They sat in the growing dark. Fred was cold. He got up and walked around, crossed his arms, rubbed his hands. What *was* his problem? Only that both his parents had given him away, left him for new-model families. At least Jess let him live with her. But she cooked stuff he didn't like, listened to music he didn't like, and she was moody, like depressed or something. How could she be happy, sitting in her studio all day and drawing things like a little kid. And every single day he thought of what he'd overheard that morning when he'd left for school and went back for his earbuds. Jess didn't know he was there, she was on the phone and she said – Fred could remember it word for word, he even wrote it down later, trying to somehow hold it instead of it holding him – she said, 'Just because I wanted children of my own doesn't mean that I'm happy to take her reject. I didn't want just any kid, I wanted my own kid.'

Fred shook his head, trying to get rid of the memory. He felt a bit dizzy after skolling basically a whole can.

'So which one's your real mum?' he asked Ash.

'They both love me.'

Fred finished the last drops, crushed the can under his foot.

'I'm proud of them,' Ash added suddenly, because he was, and he wanted to defend them. They were good people, who did good things. They had this thing they said: 'Don't judge; think, instead.' Ash really tried to live by that. They encouraged him to see the world from others' points of view, to give everyone a go. It was one of the reasons Ash had tried to be a friend to Fred, the new kid . . . Ash's family felt right. Him, Eloise, Jamie, Paul, it felt normal, good. So why was he having to justify himself, his family, to Fred?

'What about your family?' Ash asked. He knew Fred wasn't living with either of his parents.

'They're in Melbourne,' was all Fred could come up with to say. He didn't know how to tell that story, couldn't see it, give it shape. Fred's family didn't feel right. And they didn't make him feel right. They made him feel incompetent. Unwanted.

Laila sat down next to Ash. 'It's getting really cold,' she said, rubbing her arms. It had also become quite dark now, but no one mentioned that. Ash felt grateful to Laila, she had stood up for him, she was quiet but she wasn't afraid to say what she thought.

'I wish I had the tourmaline stone,' said Laila.

Chrystal got out her candy. She offered some to Fred.

'Yum,' said Fred, 'Reese's Peanut Butter.' But it was so sweet and chalky, and it stuck to the roof of his mouth. Hard to swallow. He actually felt a bit sick. Maybe it was the drink on an empty stomach.

'It's American candy,' said Chrystal. 'The candy I like.'

Laila wouldn't have eaten it anyway, she was a nuts and seeds person.

Ash ate another apple.

Laila stood up, lifted her arms to the sky, swept them down. Fred laughed, but she didn't seem to care. She'd taken off her beanie, and was touching her long hair, putting it up in her scarf, taking it down again, running her fingers through it. 'I hope Elle'll be able to see the bag in the dark. See where you left it.'

Laila made a turban from her scarf, a few strands of hair hung in waves around her neck, down her back. She sat down again, shivered.

'You know our eyes adjust to the dark,' said Ash. 'It's called dark adaptation.' He threw his apple core into the bush for the kangaroos. 'Some animals have evolved to live in total darkness. Some fish have.'

'Total darkness,' said Fred. 'Cool.' It was a stupid thing to say, but he didn't want Ash to hate him.

'And the night sky,' Ash looked up, 'it's actually blue.'

'Yeah sometimes it looks dark blue,' said Fred. 'We only see it as dark because of our eyes.' Jess had told him that. 'It's the same regular blue sky, but with no sun shining on it.' Fred looked up too, felt the blood rush to his head as he made out the sharp black outlines of the leaves, the branches like skeletons against a grey mist.

'I wonder when we'll see the moon,' said Laila.

'What's it called again? A supermoon?' said Fred.

'Yeah it's when the moon's closest to Earth,' said Ash. 'That's why it's brighter. You always get them around Easter.'

'And the king tides,' added Laila.

'Sounds like a Marvel character,' laughed Fred. 'Supermoon!'

'The way to see in the dark, you're supposed to let yourself adjust for thirty minutes,' said Ash. 'Humans can see in bright sunlight, and also in nearly total darkness. We don't actually need that much light to see.'

As if the world had heard them, the light seemed to dim suddenly.

Ash stood, reached out and touched the rust-coloured, papery bark at the base of a mountain ash. It steadied him, somehow.

Fred stumbled.

Chrystal hummed.

Looked up.

'Where are the birds now?'

•

Elle was jogging at a good pace down the track. Now that she wasn't hampered by the others, she could take off, go fast.

Elle was a good runner. She was fit and strong, had done taekwondo since she was six. It was amazing how quickly you warmed up when running, even when the weather was cold. She took off her high-vis and tied it around her waist. If she'd been wearing proper running gear, she could have gone faster. And if she'd strapped her knee. Elle had done her ACL eight months earlier, playing soccer. She wasn't really supposed to run too far.

She had to keep her eyes on the ground so she didn't stumble or roll her ankle on tree roots or rocks. She had a weakness there; she'd rolled her right ankle before and it had never totally mended. This wasn't a track meant for running. And it was hard to see. The air was cold now, but Elle's face, her skin, was hot.

A big, black kangaroo bounded across the track. Elle felt it under her feet, the vibration.

It started to rain just as she reached the bend in the track with the burnt trees where Fred had left the stuff. She'd be able to spot the white of the plastic bag, shimmering in the rain, she almost imagined it.

She was sweating, could feel it turning cold on her back.

Somewhere in the forest, a kookaburra laughed.

Elle reached the tree stump, the rocks.

The bag was gone.

Seven

'How long has it been?'

Ash stood up. Stretched. 'Hard to tell. An hour? Over an hour?'

'I reckon it must be seven o'clock,' said Laila. 'Look how dark it's got.'

'She should be back by now.' Ash looked in the direction Elle had run. 'Doesn't Elle have that knee injury?' I should have gone, he thought, should have insisted.

Or at least offered.

They heard the mournful cry of another black cockatoo. The air shifted, wind dropped.

'All the birds have gone to shelter,' said Laila into the silence.

Ash heard it, a pitter patter on his jacket. Light rain was falling.

'We should try to keep dry,' he told the others.

'It's hardly even raining.'

Ash ignored Fred. 'Let's get under that tree.'

The four of them put their packs in the hollow of a huge mountain ash. The base of the tree was wide, the roots like a buttress, and the brown bark rough and thick, like a big shaggy animal, but at the top it looked smooth and pale in the fading, cloudy light.

Ash felt a cold drop on his face. The trees had dark-pink water stains running down their grey trunks like they were bleeding. The rain, almost like mist, was now surrounding them. Ash was aware of Laila next to him, their shoulders almost touching. The soft rain made the four of them quiet. Laila held out her hand so that each leaf of a tree fern brushed against it, water droplets falling. Laila was always reaching out, but Chrystal was the opposite. She seemed to avoid touching people. She didn't hug, didn't touch your arm, anything like that, just pulled at her hair. That must hurt, thought Ash. She would be a hard person to comfort.

'See, Chrystal,' he reassured her, 'not a storm, just rain.'

'We'll be able to see her head torch when she comes up the hill.' Laila squinted in the twilight.

'Hang on, is that her?'

'What?'

'Did you hear her?'

It was so easy to imagine you saw something, heard something. Did Ash see a light bobbing up and down through the trees?

Rain on the leaves shimmered silvery grey.

'Is that her high-vis?' said Fred, peering into the forest.

A few seconds later, Elle came puffing up the track. She limped slightly, her skin glistened, her long ponytail golden in the last little glints of light.

'Why didn't you use a head torch?' said Ash.

'It wasn't there,' puffed Elle, her eyes shining. Prussian Blue, Fred saw the colour.

'It was gone, the whole bag was gone.' She bent over, hands on her knees, to get her breath.

'Oh great,' said Fred, 'someone took my stash.'

Elle raised her head. 'And our torches and the phone.' She felt the back of her knee, her hamstring. Took a breath. 'The compass.' Another breath. 'And map.'

He could apologise, thought Ash. Instead, Fred said, 'Why did you make me leave it there?'

'Why did you bring that stuff in the first place?' said Ash. He couldn't help himself. 'This never would have happened.'

'We can't blame each other, guys,' said Laila, 'it makes a bad energy. I think we should form the circle, get our connection back.'

'I'm not going in another freaking circle!' said Fred. Jesus, get in the real world.

The five of them stood in the rain.

'Maybe another group picked it up,' said Elle. She was puffing, hands on hips, squinting at the sky, not sure what to do next.

'Why can't you say I'm sorry?' Ash asked Fred. 'It won't kill you. You'll be the same person after you've said those two words.'

Fred looked so angry, his small face pinched and hard, his chin jutting. Inside he was screaming. Sorry! Sorry I'm such a terrible person, sorry that I'm so stupid, sorry that I wrecked your great group, your circle of energy. You're right, I'm blind Freddy. I can't do anything right. SORRY!

But he said nothing. Just scowled.

'Let's not worry about that,' said Elle, breathing out heavily, trying to regain some control. 'Okay, we don't have a torch and we don't have a compass or phone. Or the map.' She had to think quickly, rationally. 'Who votes we go back to where the bus dropped us off. Do you reckon an adult will be there? They said an adult wouldn't be far away.'

'Let's not turn back,' said Ash. 'We mightn't even be able to find the starting place.'

'True,' said Elle. 'Who votes we keep going?'

Everyone did. Phew. They were united in that.

Laila was beside Elle. 'What did the note in the bucket say?'

Elle got it out of her pocket. 'Walk north to the top of the next ridge. Up the hill has to be north, don't you reckon? I say we head up the hill and try to go by the hints in the buckets. And I have the light on Dad's watch. Laila, you know the area best. Do you think north is up this way?'

Laila was fishing around for a stone in her cloth bag.

Fred peered at the watch. 'What a piece of crap!'

'Yes, whatever, it's a light, Fred. It's all we've got.' Thanks to you, she felt like adding. Elle was getting very sick of his annoying comments.

Chrystal was plonked on the ground near the tree. 'Come on, Chrystal, don't sit in the wet, you'll get really cold.' Elle reached out her hand. Chrystal still sat.

It's because you're unfit that you're so slow, thought Elle crossly. You never exercise and all you do is eat chips, cheese and white bread. But she knew it was useless thinking mean thoughts about Chrystal. Elle also knew that if you give people a job, like a role, make them feel important, they can respond. She went over to Fred.

'Can you get her to walk with you? She likes you. Please?'

He stood there, nothing but tight anger.

If she kept talking, would it make him more or less likely to help? Elle took a risk . . .

'It's something you could do for us. For the group.'

Fred didn't move for a moment. Then he went over, reached out his hand to help her up. Chrystal hesitated, then took it.

'So which way do we go, do you reckon?' said Ash. 'This is going to be really hard with no map or torches.'

Laila held a stone and looked up at the sky, which made Elle wonder whether Laila had any idea where they were, or which way was which.

'Hopefully when the moon rises more, it'll give us some light,' said Ash.

'Except it's cloudy up there,' said Elle.

'Yeah,' said Ash, 'I can't see it yet.'

Elle checked the time: 7:10. She took a deep breath. 'Laila? This way, do you reckon?'

'What about the stars?' said Laila. 'Like the Southern Cross.'

Okay, she's got absolutely no idea, thought Elle. Everyone was letting her down. But at that moment, the clouds moved and revealed the moon through the trees, quite low in the sky but so full and bright. She gasped. 'Look.'

'It's huge,' said Laila.

They all watched. The moon glowed yellow, the colour of butter.

In a patch of cloudless sky, a solitary star appeared.

'There's the evening star, that comes out first, doesn't it?' said Elle. 'Which part of the sky is it in?'

But clouds swept across and covered it.

'Did you reckon we were on the Pennyroyal Ridge, Laila?' Think, Laila! Elle wanted to add. Don't just stand there staring at the sky! Use your brain! Where are we?

'Yeah, we might be,' said Laila with no certainty at all. 'I think we go over this ridge, then we'll be in the valley that school looks over. We might see the lights of school on the other side when we get to the top.'

'So this way is north, do you think?' said Elle.

Laila didn't give a direct answer. 'If we can see lights, or the ocean, we'll get our bearings.'

'I don't know how we'll see the ocean,' said Elle. 'It's too dark now. But the note said go to the top of the next ridge, so it would definitely be uphill.'

Laila agreed, and slowly, they made their way up, hopefully heading north.

'I reckon we're going in the right direction,' said Elle, trying to reassure the others. It was harder to walk in the dark, and the rain; they'd have to be careful that they didn't get injured.

'I'm sick of all this climbing,' Fred puffed. 'Aren't there any downhill parts of this bloody hike?' He stopped to get his breath. 'I wish I had my phone. It's stupid that we had to hand them in.'

'We did have a phone, Fred,' said Elle, pointedly.

It was strange for all of them, not being able to reach automatically for their phone. A phone was like an extension of your arm. You were never alone; it was always with you. Except sometimes Elle didn't take it when she went for a run. Because no matter what you were thinking, or doing, no matter where you were, your phone would always demand your attention. But now, they had nothing. Only themselves. Maybe this was exactly what Johan wanted.

'There it is,' said Ash as they came to some rough, wide steps cut into the track, 'the Southern Cross! Look, the clouds are moving.'

The clouds had cleared part of the sky, and the night shone silver.

'Wow, how bright is it,' said Ash.

The moon cast a light everywhere.

'Does it point south?' asked Fred.

'Hang on, I know what to do,' said Ash. 'You imagine a line running from the top to the foot of the cross. A diagonal line like this, across the sky.' He lifted his arm and pointed. 'Then you keep that line going for four times the length of the cross. Then go vertically straight down to the horizon. That way is south.'

They all tried to do what Ash said, pointing into the murky sky. But the clouds must have been racing up there because the stars and the Southern Cross kept disappearing. 'Is that even the Southern Cross?' asked Fred.

'I reckon we go,' Ash swung around, still pointing, 'that way. North.'

It was like they were playing a little kids' game, where you had to close your eyes and spin around.

The soft rain was getting heavier.

Chrystal was standing apart from them, hugging herself, shivering, making her bizarre noise, a constant tense murmur, a drone.

Elle called, 'Chrystal, are you okay?'

'My headache,' she said, 'something's coming.'

They ignored Chrystal's headache, and walked into the night, heading in the direction they still hoped was north. 'You need to stay near us,' Elle told Chrystal. 'I know you don't want to, but we need to hold on to each other.'

They trampled on, wet and cold and unsure. Elle went first, Fred held her arm, then Ash held Fred's, Laila held Ash's and Chrystal held Laila's oilskin coat because she wouldn't hold her arm.

The path was rocky, they tripped and stumbled. 'It's like we're blind,' said Laila.

'That's what my dad calls me.' Fred laughed into the darkness. 'Blind Freddy.' He paused. 'When actually I have really good eyesight.'

It was true. He'd had it tested when he stopped focusing at school.

Ash was about to ask again where Fred's dad was, when suddenly Chrystal spoke.

'You're not blind.'

'I know I'm not blind, idiot.'

Elle stopped, so everyone stopped, half bumping into each other. 'She's not an idiot.'

'I've got news for you,' said Fred. 'She's a Year Nine who only eats white food, won't wear a jacket when it's raining and talks to her Snoopy toy.'

'Shut up, Fred,' said Ash. 'Don't talk about Chrystal as if she's not here.'

'Ever heard of personal space?' Fred said nastily to Laila, who had ended up close to him when they had all stopped on the track. Laila ignored him, but Ash had an urge to shove Fred so that he'd fall from the track, backwards into the rocks and tree roots and darkness. He blocked that thought out, so that he didn't even know he had it.

They'd let go of each other. Elle was worried that things were falling apart. She tried to focus. What does the team need from me now? How can I guide them safely out of here and to school? She checked the watch. 'It's seven forty-five now. We'll be okay, we can just get up this ridge, then we can find the bucket. It's probably downhill from there. Down to school.'

'How will we find the bucket in the dark?' said Ash.

'Look, even when the moon's behind the clouds, we can still see.' Behind the clouds was a foggy circle, the supermoon, a diffused light like a misty screen in the gloom. And every now and then, the moon did break through the clouds. It was getting smaller as it rose, but still very bright, lighting the clouds so that they gleamed silver, and the sky looked almost blue behind them.

'Even if we can't find the bucket, I'm sure we'll see lights or something to help us get our bearings.'

They came to the top of another hill. Rain was falling evenly now. Is this the next ridge? Elle wondered. From the note? There were no lights. No sign of the school, a road, a house. Or anything else.

'How long since the last bucket?' said Ash. 'It didn't say a distance to walk.' The next ridge could be anywhere. They were getting really wet. 'This is a kind of clearing. It could be here?' Ash felt Laila's hand back around his arm.

'The last two were in clearings,' added Laila.

Elle pressed the light on her watch in the rain. She bent down, peering around at knee level.

'I've found it!' Ash was holding a bucket. 'Omigod, I found it!'

'Ash! Yes!'

'My eyes have adjusted. And the moon's so bright.'

There it was, the number 3 on the side. They had reached bucket three!

'How did we even do that?' said Laila.

'Now we know we're still on the right track. Well done, Laila! And Ash! We did walk north!' They all felt so relieved. 'Lucky you've got a good sense of direction.'

Elle leant over and picked up the note. It was in a plastic pocket, but it was hard to read because there was water in the bottom of the bucket.

'Continue north-west for approximately seven kilometres.' She folded it neatly and put it in her pocket with the other notes.

'Okay, so we were heading north, so north-west we veer to the left. The track seems to head in that direction.' Elle would save the day. And they'd make it even without a compass. They'd be heroes! She'd be a hero!

'Hey, look!' Fred picked up something bright in the moon-light. Was it fungi, a mushroom? Elle came over and held her watch close to Fred's hand.

'It's popcorn!' Fred laughed. It was a relief to come across something so domestic, something that suggested they weren't really out in the wild on their own. And something as innocent, as fun as popcorn. It made Fred think of the movies, a crowded cinema in the city before Covid. 'There must be other people around,' he said. 'We're not alone at all. There's probably a teacher munching on popcorn really close by. Johan!' He called out. 'Sammi! I see you! Hey, can you give us a hint? We've lost our compass!'

'Don't tell them that,' said Elle. 'We need to find our own way, not have them rescue us.'

'Hey, here's another bit. We could follow the popcorn,' said Fred, 'like Hansel and Gretel.'

'Yeah.' Ash laughed. 'But didn't they end up being locked up and starved or something?'

They walked on. Okay, it was raining, but they were on the right track, and the moon was bright enough to see a few steps ahead. Finding the popcorn had kind of lightened the mood – they were able to joke about scary stories they remembered from when they were kids.

Laila knew them all. 'It's all we read,' she said, 'fairy tales, myths and legends, we had no other books at all.'

'That's the opposite of me,' said Ash, 'I only had the new ones.' He'd always been given books that featured two mothers when he was little, by well-meaning friends and relatives, no stories about evil stepmothers or children lost in the woods.

'This thing happened in Stockholm that was like a fairy tale,' said Elle.

'What, like the Pied Piper of Hamelin?' asked Laila. 'You know that's a true story?'

'What? I don't think so,' said Elle. 'Anyway, I'm not talking about an old story. This happened in Stockholm when I lived there, like four years ago. These children, they were refugees and being sent back to their country by the Swedish government.'

'That doesn't sound like a fairy tale,' said Ash.

'Wait,' said Elle, 'it was. They developed this thing where they went into a coma after they were told they were being deported. Like there was no medical explanation for it, but it was a full-on coma. It always reminded me of Sleeping Beauty. I'm sure she went to sleep for one hundred years?'

'My dad would call that a physical reaction to a psychological situation,' said Laila. 'He loves stories like that.'

Fred wondered what his dad would call it. It was like dealing with something by not feeling it. The moon was so bright now that when Fred looked at it he had to squint, almost like staring at the sun.

Elle noticed a star through the clouds, out of focus, a small intense spark of light. 'Resignation syndrome, it was called.' She remembered the Swedish word because it sounded so much like giving up. *Uppgivenhetssyndrom.*

'You know the first fairy tales were for adults?' said Laila.

'Doesn't surprise me,' said Ash. 'They're pretty brutal. Wasn't the witch in Hansel and Gretel fattening one of them up to eat them?'

'And in Sleeping Beauty,' continued Laila, 'there was cannibalism, and rape.'

No one knew quite what to say about that. Not the Disney fairy tales, but darker, brutal stories – about anger, aggression, lust, violence, jealousy; emotions it was hard to admit you felt.

'What was the one about the little man, and people had to guess his name?' asked Fred after a while.

'Rumpelstiltskin.'

'Yeah, that's right!'

Laila started to tell the story. 'Once there was a tiny man,' she began, 'whose name was hidden in the forest . . .' She was a great storyteller, her deep voice was mesmerising, and while she spoke, they followed her. The bright moon cast long shadows of darkness, and no one noticed that the track seemed to be winding around, almost doing a U-turn.

Until, 'Hang on,' Laila interrupted her own story, 'it feels like we're going back the other way. Have we changed direction?'

'It does actually,' said Ash. 'Did anyone see another track that we could have taken, heading north-west?'

'It's hard to see,' said Elle, 'without a torch. But Johan did say that some of the walking would be on older tracks, more overgrown, and harder to follow. Didn't he?'

'We might have missed a track to the left earlier,' said Ash, as they walked slowly on. 'Let's see if we can find one.'

'To continue north-west, I reckon we need to go that way.' Elle pointed left. 'We walked north and we know that was the right direction because we came to the bucket. So heading west would definitely be continuing left. North-west.'

'But it's like we've turned around,' said Laila.

If only we had a compass, thought Ash, but he stayed quiet.

'Okay then,' said Laila, 'are you saying we should leave the track here?'

'What do you think, Ash?' asked Elle.

'I suppose,' said Ash. 'If you think this is the right direction? Let's go a bit further and see if there's any path?'

They continued on a little way. It was hard to see what was a track and what was just a bit of forest that wasn't as dense. 'Is this a track?' Ash asked.

'Maybe,' said Elle. 'Come on, let's try it.' And they veered left.

If it was a track, it soon seemed to come to an end, and the bush took over again. The ground was uneven. Sometimes it was so dense they had to scramble around whole walls of scrub, vines, rocks, undergrowth.

Laila didn't pick up the story again because they needed to concentrate. Branches, bracken and ferns scratched them, they had to climb over logs and circle around trees.

'I don't think Johan meant walk on no track at all,' said Ash. He stopped. 'I don't think this is right.'

Every few minutes, the moon escaped from behind the clouds and lit up their surroundings. 'See what I mean,' said Elle, 'it's not dark at all when the moon comes out.' Mud glistened, droplets of rain shone and sparkled, the flat surface of gum leaves reflected the rain in the moonlight. Elle's knee was hurting. They stopped to wait for Chrystal.

'Look,' said Ash. The moon was getting brighter, casting their own shadows quite sharply on the ground.

They came to a huge boulder, like a bulky animal silhouetted against the sky, and another track. It was very rough, but it seemed to be heading in the direction they hoped was north-west. 'I reckon this is the one we're supposed to be on,' said Elle. 'The one we missed.' No one disagreed, and it was a relief to be back on a track and not bush-bashing their way in the dark anymore, but this new path twisted and turned, went uphill and down, like the path of a rollercoaster. Even if they'd been heading north-west originally, they had lost any sense of direction now.

'Do you think we're still going north-west?' Ash asked after a while.

'Hard to know,' said Elle.

'This is so steep,' complained Fred. 'And the puddles at the bottom, they're deep.'

'Yeah but the rain's not that heavy,' said Elle. Still, everyone was soaking wet now, and getting tired. Elle thought if the rain eased off a bit or they found a shelter, they could stop for a few minutes. She could pass around her choc-chip cookies, that would cheer them up.

They came to another clearing, where this new track seemed to finish. When they were in open ground, it was even lighter because the moon wasn't so blocked by trees. 'Look for a bucket,' said Elle.

'Have we gone seven ks though? I don't think we would have walked that far,' said Ash.

They could make out forms of darker and lighter space, the black trees outlined against the velvety grey sky. The trees made patterns on the clouds behind them.

There was a big solid mass beyond the trees in front of them. Was it the ocean? 'Can you smell the sea,' asked Ash, 'if you turn this way?'

'All I can smell is rain,' said Laila.

They searched around for the bucket.

'I think I can see it!' called Ash. 'Yes! Over here.'

'Ash, you are the best at finding buckets!'

'We got here quickly!' said Ash. 'Was that seven ks?'

'Maybe we took a short cut when we went through the bush,' said Elle, peering at the bucket in Ash's hands. 'Check that it's number four.'

Ash turned it around. 'Where's the number?'

'Get the note,' said Elle. It was hard to read. Elle was glad for her dad's watch. She crouched down, held the light up to the piece of paper. 'Want me to hold it?' said Ash, but Elle ignored him. She squinted, and read out the words.

'If you have found this bucket, you have . . .' she tilted the paper to the moonlight '. . . gone the wrong way.'

Eight

Oh.

All their bravado left them.

Elle stood up. The rain got heavier. 'How could we have gone the wrong way?'

'We must have missed a fork in that rough track in the dark? Do you reckon we've gone north-east, not north-west?' Ash wished he had one of his friends from the community with him. They were so good with direction, even though they never used left and right.

'Can I read it?' Ash asked.

'Ash, I read it correctly.' She really didn't need Ash questioning her judgement.

Elle pushed back her hood, wiped the rain from her forehead. 'I reckon we should go back to the last bucket, the third one, and then go left and head up that way. Stay on that first track, even if it seems to be heading back. Maybe it swings around again. Remember how Sammi said we should backtrack if we come to a bucket that tells us we've gone the wrong way?'

Elle sighed. This was the second time she was having to turn back. She checked the time. 8:56.

'Look, here's a better track,' said Fred from a bit of a distance away. 'I reckon we take this one.'

'No, Fred,' said Elle. 'We need to go back to the third bucket. I reckon we were going north-west but we got confused when the path turned us around. They must have thought some people might make this mistake, because they've put this bucket here.'

'Yeah, but if you reckon we should have branched off more to the left, we can do that from here,' said Fred.

'I don't know, Fred. We're safer to retrace our steps. That way we're not going to get totally lost.'

'But this is a track, a path, shouldn't we stay on a track?'

'Not if we have no idea where it's going! It could be the wrong track!'

Part of Elle thought, What would they do if they got back to the bucket and then went a different wrong way? At least Fred's way was a defined track. Would it lead somewhere?

'What do you think, Laila?'

'Don't ask her,' snapped Fred, 'it was her great sense of direction that got us here in the first place.'

'I never said I knew exactly where we were,' said Laila. 'I was trying to get my bearings.'

'So much for your crystals and your cosmic energy guiding you.'

'She's trying, Fred. We're all trying.' Elle wanted to add, And it's your fault we're in this situation.

'Okay,' she said, 'let's take a break, just for a few minutes, and have something to eat. Then we head back to bucket three and start again from there.' Elle took her pack over to the base of a tree, not that it really offered much shelter but it was better than standing out in the open in the rain. She got the cookies, and the cookie dough for Chrystal, out of her pack. Raindrops spattered on the plastic bag.

There was a click of a can opening.

'What? Where did you get that from?' said Ash.

'I said he could take one,' said Elle.

'But he had one when you went back for the stuff.'

'What?'

'This is his second can.'

'Thanks a lot.' Fred shoved Ash.

'Fred, we agreed on one,' said Elle. He was such a wrecker.

Who was she? Fred thought angrily. His mother? 'I found another one at the bottom of my bag. Want some?'

Elle turned her back. He was that kind of person. Always pushing. One can was never going to be enough.

'Fred,' she said, 'please don't drink it. I'm the leader.'

'I'm the leader,' he mimicked her. 'Want some, Chrystal?'

'I guess.'

'Don't give it to her. Fred, can you tip it out? You had one, that's what we said –'

Fred handed the can to Chrystal, it caught the moonlight as she sipped at it.

'Fred,' said Elle, 'can you just do what someone asks you to? Once? Like it won't kill you.'

But Fred felt it almost would. It was somehow giving ground, giving something of himself away, something that he couldn't give.

They ate the cookies. Fred drank from the can. He'd had two drinks now, and no food. Would he get drunk? He was small, too, it didn't take much for smaller people to get drunk. What could Elle do? Wrestle him to the ground and grab it off him? And Chrystal was an idiot to drink some, but a couple of sips wasn't going to be a big problem.

'What do you reckon, Laila? We go back the way we came?' Laila knew the area best, and Elle could count on her to be sensible.

Laila took out a stone from her little bag. Held it. 'Um, I'm not really sure.'

'Can't your stones help you now?' Fred laughed.

'Hey, shut up.' Ash was close to Fred before he knew it.

'Oooh, defending your girlfriend.'

'I said shut up, Fred.'

'You told me you thought she was hot.'

'No, you told me. You said that.'

'I'm glad you two were discussing Laila like that, objectifying her,' said Elle. 'How do you think that makes her feel?'

Laila held the stone, rubbed it in her hand.

'It'd make Laila feel good, wouldn't it?' Fred said belligerently. 'If people thought she was hot?'

Laila ignored them.

Ash glared at Fred in the moonlight.

'Jesus, Ash, stop looking at me like a dad. Why don't you say what you really think? Just say what you think.'

Something snapped in Ash. 'I think you're being a dickhead. To her, to me, to all of us.' His voice got louder. 'I don't know what your problem is, but I think you're being a real arsehole.' He muttered to himself, 'I never knew you were such an arsehole.' He shoved him. Fred stumbled. 'Why can't you shut up?' Ash turned away from them all. 'That's what I think.'

No one said anything. This was Ash. Friendly, good-natured Ash.

Rain splashed down around them.

'Not such a nice guy now, are you?' said Fred, smiling.

But Ash took a deep breath, held his stone in his pocket. It made him feel strong. 'Just leave her alone,' he said. 'Leave us all alone.'

'Okay,' said Fred, 'I will.' He picked up his pack and started to march up the hill.

'Hey, I don't mean go off on your own.'

'You want me to leave you all alone?' said Fred without turning around. 'That's what you just said. Then that's what I'll do.'

'Fred, don't be such a pain. Come on.'

'That's not what Ash meant,' said Elle, heading up towards Fred. 'He meant stop being such a . . . stop hanging shit on everyone.'

'This is because of you!' Laila's voice was losing its mellow tone. 'If we had the compass and the map and the torches, we'd be fine.' She undid her scarf, it was too wet. 'This would have been fun.'

Elle was beginning to wish she'd let Fred keep the stupid cans. At least then they'd still have the stuff they really needed. If she hadn't tried to assert herself, throw her weight around . . .

'Listen, guys, there's no point fighting about it. Let's just go back to the last bucket, and start again from there . . . It's dark, Fred, you can't go off on your own.'

She could feel Chrystal, her body vibrating, humming, tense beside her.

Fred ignored Elle. 'Who's coming with me?' he demanded. His small silhouette didn't budge.

'Fred, where are you going? Where will you go?' Elle needed him to stay with them.

He crushed the can, threw it on the ground towards them.

'Don't!' said Elle. 'Pick that up.' She was losing control of the group.

He wasn't going to, so Elle did. She couldn't walk past rubbish and leave it there.

'Fred,' she said, trying to reason with him, 'we can't get more lost than we already are. We need to go back to the bucket. It's the logical thing to –'

'It's stupid to go back,' Fred interrupted her. 'I say we head this way. We'll come to that road to Apollo Bay, or Elliot Ridge.'

'Fred, we need to stay together.'

But he had already turned away. 'See ya.'

Fred went up the hill.

Ash felt anger fill up inside him. He was bigger than Fred, stronger. He could grab Fred, make him come with them. Part of him wanted to do that. But Ash hated violence. He knew he did.

'Fred!' he yelled.

'Leave him,' said Elle.

'But that's the main rule, Elle. Don't separate.'

'Fred,' Ash called one more time, 'please, come back.' They could hardly see him now.

Fred was almost running. 'I'll get back before you!' he shouted.

'I can't hear you,' said Chrystal, agitated. 'I can't hear you properly.'

Hearing Chrystal's voice, Fred stopped at the top of the track.

'Chrystal,' he called, 'want to come with me?'

Chrystal didn't move. 'Stay with us,' said Elle quietly.

'This is a short cut, Chrystal. I'm taking a short cut.' Fred took a few steps back towards them.

Chrystal started plodding up the hill after him.

'Come back!' shouted Elle, getting desperate now. 'Chrystal, we need to stay together. He doesn't know where he's going!'

'Elle,' Laila held Elle's arm, 'just leave them.'

'I'm the leader,' Elle said, almost in tears. She thought of what her dad said, she couldn't let Chrystal go, it was irresponsible! 'Remember, we all agreed.'

But she let Laila lead her back down the track, away from Fred and Chrystal, because she'd run out of options, and didn't know what else to do.

Before they'd even started down the hill again, Chrystal was calling for them to wait.

'He was too fast for me,' she said when she caught up.

'I'm really glad you've come back,' said Elle, zipping up her pack. 'Thanks, Chrystal.'

And off they set, minus one, into the dark, back to the third bucket.

•

Fred marched on, up and over the ridge.

He was so sick of people telling him what to do. And that Elle, what a know-all. There were kids like that at Grammar, too. Lived all over the world, spoke three languages, thought they owned the place. 'When I lived here, when I lived there.' Fred had only lived in Melbourne, until he was chucked away to boarding school, and then, when he stuffed that up, here with his aunty.

He reached the top of the hill. The path stopped. Good, he thought angrily, he could invent his own short cut.

He wished he had his phone, his music, torch.

But it was a bit lighter here, the moon was higher now. Brighter.

It was getting windier, too.

Running up the hill had made him puffed, so he sat on a rock. It was wet, but the rain had stopped again.

Fred opened his backpack and unwrapped a sandwich that Jess had made for him. Jess who didn't like him, who'd wanted a kid of her own.

Fred's mum only had one kid. Him. He was a disappointment to her. To both his parents. Fred felt so angry – that he was here with these stupid people in the stupid bush in the cold and the dark, and its prickly grasses and spiky ferns, its hard rocks and steep tracks and that wind that came up over the ridge. Elle was such a pain. And Ash was a yes-man, he agreed with everything she said.

In the moonlight, Fred could see the grey of the clouds moving fast above him. They seemed close. Now rain was starting again. Bloody rain, it was getting heavier. Suddenly it would come across in angles, like it was being thrown at him, wind surging through the tops of the trees.

Fred finished his sandwich quickly, it was getting wet in his hands, then he ate the muffin and the banana that Jess had packed. There was only a protein bar left. He ate most of that, too. Not much water left, either. But hang on, he had a lighter! In the side pocket of his backpack. They used to sneak outside the boarding house and smoke. Fred didn't smoke, he didn't like it, but he had the lighter!

He flicked it. On, off, on, off. Each time it went off, he could see less, and his eyes had to adjust to the darkness again. What had Ash called it? He flicked it on, stood up, tried to see if there was another track somewhere. It was hopeless, because he could only see one step ahead and, around that, rain falling through the flame, and a halo of darkness. It was almost easier to use the moonlight because looking at the flame made everything around it go black.

But once his eyes adjusted, Fred did see, on the ground in front of him, a small pink runner.

Where had that come from? Must be a clue they left, like the buckets, thought Fred, and I need to find the other one. No one said there'd be clues like this. Hah! Looks like I am on the right track, idiots. Fred picked it up. It was wet, dirty, but not dirty as if it had been there for ages. It looked quite new. It was way too small for someone in Year Nine. It reminded Fred of his dad's two new children in Melbourne, little kids who were still good and sweet and cute. Hannah and Hamish. Not his dad's actual children. But they may as well be. His dad lived with children who weren't his, and had sent his own child away. Who knows, his dad might even have a kid with Louise. She was young enough. She could already be pregnant. His dad probably wouldn't even tell him. Fred wished he had another can.

He decided to wait for the rain to stop. He tried to find shelter, but even under the trees, water dripped onto him. He flicked the lighter on. It made him feel warmer, and braver. Then the wind blew it out. He wished he had a compass, but even after two terms at Bellarine, where they did heaps of outdoor ed, he'd always left that for others to do, so he still couldn't read a compass properly. Blind Freddy.

Fred stared out at the undergrowth. It looked ghostly in the moonlight. Sap glistened on the tree where he was sheltering. He held the lighter up to it, cupped his hand to protect the flame. Sap Green. But this sap wasn't green at all. More like Burnt Umber, Copper Beech, he could see them lined up, almost read them. He shouldn't waste the lighter fluid. It didn't feel like there was much left. The warmth of it on his hands made Fred realise how cold he was. Cold was the worst. Like so many sensations, you forget how it feels until it hits you again. Cold, heat, pain.

He felt cold, and pissed off, abandoned by them all.

He was just thinking that the rain wasn't going to stop anytime soon, so he'd better get going, try somehow to find his way back, when he saw something moving through the trees. It must be one of the other groups! 'Hey!' he called. He stood up. 'Hey!'

But it wasn't a group from school.

It was a little girl.

Nine

Nobody spoke.

The four of them continued down the track, back to the third bucket. They'd thought downhill would be easier, but it was slippery now, and hard to see very far in front of them. Elle fell into a stumbling, heavy jog which put pressure on her knee, but seemed to work better than walking. Except when it was super slippery. 'Turn side-on to the hill,' she told the others, 'and go down like a sideways step. Your feet don't slide as much.'

The wind made creaking sounds above, shadows of the gum trees swayed. Shards of bark fell from the trees, making the four of them startle. Now and again they felt a shudder under the earth, a kangaroo bounding away, unseen, somewhere.

Fred's absence was like a presence between them. They had been told to stay together, and they had broken the most important rule. And Elle was worried. Was he drunk? Did he have food? Water?

Rain was coming down hard now, their shoes slid in the mud, and strands of the stringy bark caught around their feet. They had to hold on to each other. 'Careful,' said Ash, 'it's steep here.'

Walking in mud was really slowing them down, but at last they reached the boulder, the spot where they'd met the track. They turned, and went back down through the bush, the way they had come.

'We have to retrace our steps exactly,' said Elle, 'or we'll get completely lost.' She had to hold on to the hope that they'd find the third bucket again.

It was past nine o'clock now, but strangely not as dark as it had been earlier. The moon had risen, up over the treetops, and cast its glimmering light over the forest. The wind was gusty. They'd put on their polar fleeces and slickers under their high-vis vests. Except for Chrystal. Elle had suggested she put it on a few times now. 'You'll get cold, aren't you cold? Put on the jacket.' Her mum had gone to the trouble of buying it.

'I don't wear that fabric.'

Well that's grateful. Elle pushed aside spiky grass, curtains of vines, leaves, bark, all randomly woven together.

'Mmmmmm fleecies are made from plastic. Plastic bottles. Petroleum.'

'But isn't that a good thing?' asked Ash, doing up the drawstring of his hood to stop it from falling down in the wind. 'To recycle?'

'I can smell it,' Chrystal went on. 'They melt the plastic. They force it through tiny holes to make the thread.'

'I get what you mean, Chrystal,' said Laila, 'I prefer wool.' She touched her own woollen sleeve. 'It's natural.'

'Wool is worse,' said Chrystal.

'Oh, okay right.'

'What do you wear when you get cold in America then? In Madison?' said Elle. What the hell was the right fabric for Chrystal, for god's sake.

No answer.

'I can feel it.'

'Feel the plastic? But they're really soft.'

'I hear it scratching me.' She flicked her hands, touched her face, pushing at her cheeks.

They staggered down through the bush until they reached the track that led back to the little clearing.

'I'm sure this is where it was,' said Elle. They all scrabbled around in the dark.

But there was no bucket.

'Are we in a different place?' asked Ash. He frowned in the rain.

'Do you reckon an adult comes along after us and collects the buckets?' said Laila as they stood shivering.

Elle shook her head. 'It should be here. No one would have moved it.'

'Unless we've ended up at the wrong track?' said Ash.

'But we backtracked,' said Elle, 'exactly. And remember there was a fork and a tree stump, like here. And fungi, there was fungi on the bark.'

'But every tree looks like that. There's fungi everywhere.' Ash frowned. The wind was getting stronger. 'Hey, did we leave footprints?' he asked, immediately knowing it was a stupid question, because they weren't in the desert, or the snow. And they couldn't see clearly enough if there were any footprints in the mud.

'Look.' Laila had picked something up.

Popcorn.

'See, this *is* where we were,' said Elle.

'Unless there's popcorn distributed throughout this whole bloody forest,' said Ash. 'Like in Fred's fairy tale.'

The mention of Fred made everyone quiet.

They found a few more pieces of wet, soggy popcorn in the clearing.

'Do you think someone could be following us?' Laila's green eyes reflected the moonlight. 'Or are we following someone, without realising? Another group?'

'I'm pretty sure this is where that bucket was. I don't know where it is now, but we were supposed to walk north-west for seven kilometres from here.'

'Did it say north-west?' asked Ash.

Elle checked the note. It was saturated, it felt like fabric, not paper.

'This time we have to stay on the track, and look out for any other tracks that might come off it, heading north-west. I think it was leaving this track where we went wrong.' Elle picked up her pack.

'Yeah but the track did seem to be heading back where we'd come from.'

'But it might turn around again. The tracks are so winding. Let's have something to eat and drink here and then get going again. I bet there's another track up there that we missed. We can stop for five minutes. We're supposed to take a break each hour.'

'But we must be so behind now.' Ash looked up the dark hill ahead of them. 'So much time wasted, with you having to go back, and then us going the wrong way.'

'How will we even see other tracks?' Laila added.

Elle didn't want them to get all negative. 'If we have a hot drink and a snack, we'll feel better.' It reminded Elle of Hong Kong, of her *ayi* there, whose answer to any problem was to have a hot drink and something to eat. 'We can shelter under the ferns, while it's not raining so hard. Let's do that and then head north-west.' They were already soaked through, but it still felt better without rain constantly, relentlessly falling on them.

They opened their backpacks, got out their water. Lightning flashed, a bright fork, far off.

'Wow, did you see that?'

Elle handed out cookies. 'Do you want some of the dough?' she asked Chrystal.

No answer.

I'm glad I went to the effort of bringing it for you, thought Elle.

They stood, eating the damp cookies, Chrystal humming. It wasn't exactly what Elle had imagined when she'd been baking them: sharing a fun, night-time picnic; instead they were a bedraggled, depleted little group, totally wet and almost certainly lost.

'Was that thunder?' said Laila.

'It's a long way off,' said Elle. 'See, Chrystal,' she added, 'that's the storm, out there, miles away, here it's just a bit of rain.'

Chrystal tilted her head, didn't look convinced. As if to prove her point, the rain suddenly came down harder again. Big drops hit the hoods of their jackets. They heard another crack, a boom. More thunder?

'Should we just turn back?' said Ash.

Shut up, thought Elle. It was too late, they had to go on. 'We're not turning back.'

'Right,' said Ash. 'Okay.'

'Those cookies are yum,' said Laila. 'Thanks, Elle.'

At least someone was grateful.

'I like popcorn,' said Chrystal randomly.

Ash poured hot chocolate from his thermos and handed around the keep cups. Their hands were wet and shaking as they sipped. Ash didn't even like milk much, but the warm drink made him feel a bit better. 'I reckon we'll be okay,' he said as he screwed the lid back on, 'if we just do what we planned, Elle?'

'Yeah,' said Elle. 'One step at a time.'

Ash felt bad that he'd suggested turning back. 'Hey, how good will it be when we get to school and by the fire.'

'We'll be there in maybe three hours,' said Elle. More like four, she thought but didn't say. 'Soon!'

Rain came down again. Clouds moved over the moon so that the bright light evened out, like a lamp behind a sheet.

Laila handed her empty cup to Ash. 'I wonder if Johan knew there would be this much rain.'

'Yeah,' said Ash, 'the weather's pretty bad.'

They finished their snacks and set off again. Elle took the lead. 'Let's keep on the task. I know we've had a setback but we're all good, no one's hurt and now we're heading in the direction we should be.' She swallowed. 'Except we don't have Fred with us.'

'Watch out,' said Ash, 'there are steps here.' He helped Chrystal on the slippery rocks. For a minute, she let him.

This is good, thought Elle, this is our group working together. 'Well done, everyone,' she said. Forget Fred. She needed to get a rhythm going, set a pace. Chrystal lost her balance, but Elle caught her.

Ash was also thinking of Fred, regretting that he'd got so mad at him. He shook the thought off, and tried again with Chrystal. 'Have you done much hiking? In America?' he asked her, as they traipsed on through the rain.

Chrystal didn't answer. Elle was used to Chrystal's odd habits, but Ash didn't really know Chrystal at all.

He took his hood down, maybe she hadn't heard him, his voice swallowed up in his jacket. 'I said, Have you done much hiking?' Chrystal still didn't answer.

'Chrystal?' Ash kept trying to work her out.

Humming, humming, like she was preparing to speak, warming up her vocal cords or something . . .

'My dad's an economist.'

Okay, thought Ash, that was kind of out of the blue. So do economists go hiking? Or did she mean they weren't a hiking family? He didn't follow.

Elle remembered seeing that on the form. Where they had to say something about the family. Chrystal's mum was an office manager and her dad an economist. And she had an older brother who was at college.

They walked on. Rain, no rain. Moon, no moon. Wind, then stillness. They came back to the spot where they'd left the track and headed into the bush the first time. 'So we stay on the track,' said Elle, 'and see if there are any others veering off from here.'

'He must be good at maths, then,' said Ash. 'Your dad? He'd understand the Reserve Bank and all that. Like when they printed the money a few years ago?'

'He's not working as an economist right now.'

'Oh, what does he do now?' Ash asked.

No answer.

'Mmmmmmm he's in rehab.'

Elle didn't know this. Chrystal hadn't said much about her parents at all.

'Rehab from what?' she asked, wondering if he was addicted to something.

Chrystal's shadow stopped. 'Physical rehab.'

'But like, from what?' Every answer was like drawing blood from a stone.

Chrystal tilted her head. 'Listen.'

'Yes, Chrystal, it's rain! And wind,' said Elle, frustrated. 'Just keep going, okay?'

'Hang on,' said Laila, touching Elle's arm.

Was there another sound, a truck somewhere, an engine sound, weaving through the forest?

'Is that a trailbike?' said Ash.

Now, a light, making the rain silver through the trees. There was a rough four-wheel-drive track ahead of them. 'This must be the track we should be on!' said Elle.

'It might be the teachers,' said Ash, as they all turned towards the light. Relief!

It was a spotlight, bouncing up and down. It was so dark around it that all they could see was the beam of light it made, illuminating streaks of rain, shafts of deep forest.

It was a ute, a white ute.

'That was the truck that followed us up the hill!' said Ash. 'The Hilux. Should we ask for help?'

They heard music, loud, over the engine as the ute crashed through the track.

'Let's ask if they've got a torch,' shouted Elle. That wasn't cheating, was it?

The ute roared into a clearing, not far from them. Steam rose from the exhaust, creating an eerie cloud that the brake lights shone through.

They ran over. Waved.

On the back of the ute were two dogs. Big, mixed-breed dogs. Definitely the same ute, thought Ash.

The engine stopped. Music cut out. Silence. The four of them stood in the glare of the headlights.

The motor ticked.

The driver's window was open. Against the bright lights, the inside of the ute was dark.

'Are you on your own?' He sounded like a young guy.

Elle spoke up. 'We're with a school group.'

Someone else laughed, called from inside the ute. 'Where's your teacher?'

The front-seat passenger got out, left the door open so the ute interior lit up, and around it was suddenly darker. The guy was tall, wore a lumber-jacket and a beanie, Richmond Tigers.

The bigger dog barked, once.

The guy was holding a can. Double Black.

'Can we give you a lift?' The driver leant out of the window. He wore a beanie too, plain black. He didn't look that much older than Ash.

The passenger came towards them. He staggered. Was he drunk? Elle edged closer to Ash. 'No, thanks,' she said. 'Our teacher will be here any minute.'

The guy came close to Elle. She sensed Ash moving away.

'Did you lose a phone?' His face was red and sweaty.

'We left one back there, yes . . .'

He held it out. Across the phone was a sticker. Property of Otway Community School.

'Oh, thank you, yes that's ours.' She held out her hand.

The guy smiled, lifted his arm and tossed it away, a long, strong throw. The phone arced through the air into the darkness.

Elle heard more laughter from the back of the ute, but the driver didn't seem pleased. 'What did you do that for, Sean?'

Ash could see there were four of them – the driver, this guy Sean, and two others in the back.

'That was actually our property,' said Ash. 'Property of Otway –'

'This isn't your property,' Sean swung around to Ash, 'it's my property.'

'I was talking about the phone. The property, actually it's, we're on crown land,' said Ash helpfully. 'State forest.'

Elle stood still. Where was Laila? And Chrystal?

'I bet you don't even live here. I bet you come up from bloody Geelong. Or bloody Melbourne.'

Melbourne seemed even worse than Geelong to this guy.

'No,' said Ash, trying to sound reasonable, 'we're local. We're on a hike. A school . . . hike. How about you? Hey, I go for the Tigers, too.' Ash stepped forward again, not judging, giving everyone a go.

'Going shooting.'

The guy picked up a rifle from the back of the ute. The dogs clawed and scuffled on the metal tray.

'Right, got it,' said Ash, backing away a little. 'What do you shoot?'

'Whatever.' He pointed the gun at Ash, who took a breath. 'Roos. Feral pigs. Rabbits. Scared little rabbits.' He smiled.

'Sean . . .' said the driver, and started to open his door.

'We need to keep on our hike now,' said Elle, 'so please, you go shooting and we'll keep walking.'

'We're meeting our teachers in a few minutes,' added Ash.

Sean stepped closer to Elle, reached out. 'Thanks for the free drinks.' He had a narrow face, a deep jaw and long nose. He looked like a wolf.

He nudged her in the side with the gun, pushing her.

'Don't touch me,' she said quietly.

'Sean, let's go,' the driver called.

'Don't be so uptight,' Sean said to Elle, letting the gun drop. With each step she took back, he took one towards her, like they were doing a strange dance. 'Come and have a drink in the ute. I'm happy to share. Do you like Double Black? It's a girl's drink, I reckon.'

'Come on, Sean, leave her alone.'

Ash stepped up to him. He had no idea what he would say, would do.

One of the dogs growled. Ash stopped.

'Scared of dogs, are you?'

'No.'

'Looks like you are.' Sean stepped away from Elle, his eyes on Ash now. 'You look like a girl,' he sneered.

He reached over, unclipped one of the dog's leads. It stayed on the ute, but Ash could see its muscles tense, it growled, foam around its mouth caught the moonlight. If he ran, that dog would chase him.

Sean laughed. 'Look like a girl, get treated like a girl.'

He reached out to Ash, went to grab at his long hair.

'Sean, leave them. They're kids!'

Elle stepped forward, flicked his hand away. 'Get lost, creep.'

He made to grab her, she ducked, ran, Ash ran too. Charging, tripping through the bush.

The dog was coming after him.

Someone yelled to the dog.

Elle stopped, her heart thumping. Where was Ash?

The driver yelled. 'Sean, get in, let's go.'

The Hilux roared to life again, the lights bumping through the dark trees.

'Eff off, you ugly bush pig.' Laughing, yelling. 'Get off my effing property!'

•

Elle and the others returned to the clearing.

'Shit,' said Ash, breathing hard. 'They had no right to do that.'

'Yeah, obviously, Ash.'

'This isn't his property, I don't know what he was talking about,' Ash muttered, thinking Elle was right – it was an obvious thing to say. He should have said something more to those guys, not stood frozen like a rabbit. She was so much stronger than he was.

'Where were you?' Elle asked Laila.

'I hid, out of their headlights.'

'If I'd tried to get him away from you,' Ash said, 'he would have set the dog on me. Don't you reckon?'

'Probably,' said Elle. She wasn't mad with Ash, what could he have done? 'Where's Chrystal?'

It was so hard to see now, after the bright light.

'They brought a damaging energy,' said Laila in the darkness.

'You said it, Laila,' whispered Ash.

'Yeah, toxic,' agreed Elle. 'I'm glad they've gone.'

As their eyes slowly adjusted again, they could make out more of each other's silhouettes. Elle realised she was shaking, she felt suddenly weak in her body . . . she needed to hold on to something.

Chrystal appeared from the other side of the clearing.

'There you are!' Elle was relieved.

Chrystal said nothing, but she held out her hand, open, as if she was feeding a horse.

Sitting on her palm was the compass.

•

She came close, stood in front of him. She was carrying a red bucket by its metal handle. It swung and banged against her leg, it didn't look heavy but it was big, and she was little.

He held his lighter up to her. She didn't seem frightened. Fred had got more of a fright than she had. She had a serious little face. Big eyes. Dirt smeared across one cheek like a stain. Her wet hair hung down.

'Do you know where my nanna's house is?'

'Nah.'

Where the hell had she come from?

She was walking in socks.

'Where is it! Where's Nanna's house?'

Now she was crying.

'It's okay,' said Fred. 'Stop crying.'

Still crying.

'What's in the bucket?' The number 3 was painted on its side. Helpful for some but not for Fred, now. He looked in. One shoe.

'I've got your other shoe,' said Fred.

She sniffed. 'I've been looking for that.'

He handed it to her. At least the crying had stopped.

'My shoes were hurting.' She put it in the bucket, as if she was collecting things. 'And I got a splinter.' She held out her hand, upturned, for Fred to see.

'What's your name?' the little girl asked.

'Fred. What's yours?'

'That's my grandpa's name!'

'My grandpa too. What are you doing here?'

'Going to Nanna's place. I got lost.'

Was she the kid from the bus? The one Ash said they should keep an eye on? Fred hadn't even looked at her, he wasn't sure.

'Did you get on the bus this morning?'

She nodded. She was dirty and the knee of her jeans was torn. She didn't look neat and tidy like Hannah and Hamish, although she looked about the same age as Hannah.

'Yeah, same here.'

A shot rang out. Fred jumped. A gunshot? Jesus.

'That was a big noise.'

'Yep.'

'What was that? That bang?'

'Not sure.'

'It's very cold.'

'Yep, it's cold.' Like, stating the obvious, kid.

She stood there. He sat by the tree. Looking at each other.

'I'm hungry. I want to go home.'

'You and me both.'

'Will you take me home?' Her voice wavered, like she might start crying again.

'I'm not going to leave you here, am I. I just need to work out the best way to go.'

But Fred was completely and utterly lost.

'Do you know where you live?' he asked the little girl.

'At Cumberland Point.'

'Like, the street?' Why was he even asking her this.

'My street.'

Yeah, well that's helpful.

'Do you live in Cumberland Point too?' she asked, staring at him with her big brown eyes.

'Nah . . .'

'Where do you live then?' As if everyone in the world except for Fred lived in Cumberland Point.

The question suddenly made Fred feel even more lost.

'Well I don't live in Cumberland Point.'

She looked into her Bluey backpack.

'I've run out of popcorn.'

'Do you want the rest of this?' He handed her the last bit of the protein bar.

She ate it hungrily.

Then sat down beside him.

'Mum doesn't let me have them,' she said.

'What, she thinks they're bad for you?'

''Cos I'm allergic.'

Fred's pulse quickened.

'What are you allergic to?'

She shrugged. 'Nuts.'

'How allergic?'

She looked at him like she didn't know what he was talking about.

'Do you have an EpiPen?'

She nodded earnestly. 'Mummy has that in a special bag.'

Oh great.

He held up the lighter, peered at the ingredients list on the protein bar wrapping.

Hazelnuts, peanuts, cashews.

Nuts, nuts, nuts.

Ten

'Chrystal! How did you get that?' said Ash.

'On the front seat of the truck.'

Elle wanted to throw her arms around Chrystal, but that would totally freak Chrystal out.

'Thank you!' Elle's voice came out shaky. They stood staring at the compass on Chrystal's hand.

'Chrystal, you're a genius!' said Ash.

'Not a genius.'

'Yeah, but I'm just saying, that was really quick thinking.'

'We can see north-west. Yay!' said Elle.

They turned the way the compass indicated. The rough four-wheel-drive track. Wet, shimmering leaves in the moonlight, and beyond that, deep forest, beckoning them.

'Should we look for the phone?' asked Ash. 'He threw it,' he pointed, 'that way.'

'I'll help you,' said Laila.

They all tried to look, but had no luck. 'It could be anywhere,' said Elle. 'It's impossible.'

They came back to the clearing. 'We have to trust the compass. It's the only thing we've got,' said Elle. 'I say we go this way. North-west for seven ks. Hopefully this is the track we're supposed to be on.' She pushed the light on the watch: 10:07. 'We should reach the next bucket . . . just before midnight.'

No one disagreed with her, so they took that track. After the lights of the ute, they had to get re-accustomed to the dark. 'See, dark adaptation,' said Ash. 'Takes thirty minutes.' The rain had stopped again, and Elle looked back. No one could have seen the clearing now, or even what direction they had come from. It had disappeared.

'I can't believe you got the compass,' said Ash. 'So good, Chrystal!'

Chrystal was keeping up with them now. They were walking together.

'Are you okay, Elle?' asked Laila. 'That guy was a creep.'

'Yeah, that's what I told him,' said Elle. 'I wonder where they went.'

'We'll hear them if they come back. They can't sneak up on us in a ute with spotlights,' said Ash. 'And the track here is really overgrown. I don't think a four-wheel drive could get through it.'

They could always turn off the lights, the engine. Elle knew she couldn't rely on Ash for help. On any of them. That's the thing about life, she often thought. Basically you're on your own. Elle sniffed. Lifted her head. Marched out in front. The only person who will save you is you. Elle didn't rely on anyone, not even her parents. Her brother Hughie did, but not Elle. Her friends thought she was invincible.

'Mmmmmmmm . . . you called him a creep,' said Chrystal after a while, on her own train of thought. At least she'd stopped carrying on about storms.

'Yeah, we just said that,' said Elle.

'You weren't scared.'

Believe me I was, thought Elle, but she said nothing.

'He called you ugly.' Then Chrystal looked across at Ash. 'Or you.'

'Yeah, well I don't think he was referring to Ash,' scoffed Elle. And anyway, being shouted at wasn't as scary as the fact that he was holding a gun. Still, his words had unsettled Elle. It was stupid, why would she care what that dickhead shouted at them?

'Mmmmmmm you're not ugly.'

'Thanks, Chrystal.' Elle pushed through wet ferns, trying to hold them so they didn't fling back straight into Chrystal's face. She really hoped there weren't any leeches. That was all they needed . . . not. Chrystal would freak!

'Why did he say you were ugly?'

'I don't know, Chrystal! Why do drunk idiots say the things they say? Let's not talk about it. You got our compass back, that's the main thing.' But Elle did feel weakened somehow by what that guy had said.

They kept going for a while longer, until Elle stopped. 'Hey, do you think we're heading the right way? This is hardly even a track anymore. Johan wouldn't have set this as a direction for us, I don't think?'

'It might be an old fire break, they don't all get maintained now,' said Laila. 'We should keep moving,' she added. 'There could be leeches.'

'Yeah I was thinking same,' said Elle.

Chrystal hummed, went up a note.

They seemed to be going further and further into the forest. In the moonlight they noticed another signpost by the track, but the writing was long gone. Moon spread a misty light over the trees, the path, the sign, themselves.

'You're not a bush pig. You're not a pig.'

She was fixated! 'Don't worry about it, Chrystal, it doesn't matter. They're losers.'

'You're beautiful. You look like a model. At Victoria's Secret.'

Elle snorted. Not a model!

'You could have your own YouTube channel.'

'I don't think so,' laughed Elle.

Elle wanted Chrystal to just stop going on about this stuff. But Chrystal didn't stop.

'I'm ugly.'

Elle halted. It was a sudden, sad thing to say, and Elle's instinct was to make Chrystal feel better.

'You're not ugly, Chrystal,' she said gently.

Chrystal hadn't mentioned looks before. Hers or anyone else's. Elle presumed she didn't care, because Chrystal hardly ever showered or brushed her hair. She wore no make-up and didn't seem interested in clothes. What did ugly even mean, anyway? Once you got to know a person, their looks adapted to how you thought of them. On Instagram, all beautiful meant was skinny, suntanned and symmetrical.

'Forget it, Chrystal. Come on, we need to focus on following the steps. Show me the compass.' It was on a lanyard around Chrystal's neck. 'Are we still heading north-west? It's hard to tell, to go straight.'

'Mmmmmmm I'm not easy on the eye.'

What was she on about now? Elle would have thought a phrase like this would be something Chrystal wouldn't get.

Ash and Laila had caught up. 'Are we still heading in the right direction?' asked Ash. 'This track has sort of . . . petered out.'

'We're checking the compass,' said Elle.

'I have been told that,' said Chrystal, ignoring the compass.

'Told what?' said Ash.

'Don't worry about it, Ash,' said Elle. She let go of the compass. 'It looks like we're still heading north-west.'

They walked in pairs, climbing, clambering, it was like an obstacle course.

'Easy on the eye,' Chrystal repeated, to no one.

Okay, thought Elle, someone must have explained the expression to her. And just then, a moment Elle had forgotten came back to her, of a time a while back now, when she'd been limbering up for a fun run by the Yarra in Melbourne, and she heard two men near her, and one used that expression, he'd said 'she's easy on the eye'. Elle had moved away, that had been the sensible thing to do and she'd not even thought about it. But she remembered it now, very clearly.

'That's a compliment, isn't it?' said Ash. 'Easy on the eye?'

Elle didn't want to explain to Ash why it didn't feel like a compliment. It felt like you weren't offending someone with the way you looked. But that it would be your fault if you were. Like it's your responsibility to be easy to look at. All the body image talks, the books about being proud of your body, would they ever make a difference? Elle was proud of her body, that it was strong and athletic, that her legs were long and she tanned in the summer. So did she like people to look at it? When was that right, and when was that wrong? That awful guy from the ute had upset her. But she was the leader, she had to be strong.

She turned to the others. 'If we're going in the right direction, and we walk about six ks an hour, it should take us just over an hour to get to the next bucket.'

'But we're going a lot slower than that. I reckon we're like two k an hour when it's so muddy and there's basically no track anymore,' said Laila.

The rain started again.

'When do we break?' Chrystal said.

'Not for a bit, Chrystal. I want to get to the fourth bucket by midnight. We're not even halfway yet. Bucket five is halfway. Why don't you go in front of me, lead the way? Are we still heading north-west? You need to keep checking the compass.'

Elle was behind Chrystal now. Elle's knee hurt, she shouldn't have run all that way earlier. But what choice did she have?

There was a rush overhead. 'It's windy up there.' Ash could just see the trees moving. 'I wonder where Fred is now.'

'Mmmmmmmmmm Wisconsin is part of Tornado Alley.'

'Right.' Okay that came out of nowhere. But good she'd got off that other topic.

'Tornadoes in Madison can tear the roof off a house.'

'We have cyclones here, too,' said Ash.

'Hey, Chrystal,' said Laila gently, 'storms are nature's way of healing. They break up the canopy, let light into the forest. And blow seeds around, so they can grow again.'

'Yeah,' said Ash. 'Nature has its own solutions.' But people are always trying to control nature, he thought as they bush-bashed through the rain. Not go with it, like the way they lived in the community. Ash remembered the storms in the Kimberley. They were magnificent. And the clear nights, too. Meteor showers, falling stars. He missed those nights, sleeping outside in a swag by the fire with his friends. And in the morning making damper, the warm, salty, soothing smell of it in the coals.

They traipsed on. 'Do you reckon we'll be able to find the next bucket in the moonlight?' Ash asked.

'It'll probably be in a clearing, not hidden,' said Elle. 'We don't want to miss it.'

They struggled through the bush a while longer, and came to a better track. Chrystal checked the compass. 'This is right,' Elle said. 'I think.'

Ash came over and looked as well. 'It's the right direction, anyway. Who knows if it's the right track.' Being on a wider, clearer path was easier, even in the rain and the dark. 'How long have we been walking?' he asked.

Elle pressed the watch. The light was getting weaker. 'An hour and a half, since those guys . . . since Chrystal got the compass. It's eleven forty-three.'

'We've probably done seven kilometres since that last bucket,' said Laila.

'We're so slow!' Elle could usually walk seven kilometres in under one hour!

'Watch this here, it's muddy,' she told the others as the track took them down a slope. Their shoes made squelching noises.

'Check this out,' said Ash. A giant fallen tree was across the path ahead of them. 'Hey, the bucket could be around here then.'

They couldn't see very far at all. 'They seem to put them near landmarks,' said Laila.

Then Ash called, 'Here it is! It's here!'

'Omigod, we found it! Ash, you found another one!' Elle laughed, letting the tension out. What is wrong with me? she thought. Usually, Elle had an even temperament. But now, one minute she thought she was going to start crying, the next she felt ridiculously happy and bursting with energy.

Number 4 was painted on the side in bright white paint.

'We're going to make it, guys! It doesn't matter about the time.'

'What does the note say?' said Laila.

Ash held the paper up to Elle's watch, tipping it this way and that to catch the tiny light.

'You are nearly halfway there. Head east for five kilometres.'

'Yes!' Elle pumped her fist in the air. 'We're back on track!' Their faces bright in the moonlight, Ash and Laila hugged each other with relief. Even Chrystal smiled. Elle felt so strong. Okay, they'd be late, and who knows where Fred was, but she was going to lead them out of there.

'Five ks. If we're on a track that should take us less than an hour,' she told the others.

'Check the compass.'

Chrystal held it up. Elle came close, and Chrystal didn't move away. Yes, they were a team.

'Okay . . .' Elle turned it, held it flat and straight. 'East! And we're on a track, for the moment anyway. Thanks, Chrystal.'

They got going again. 'I can't believe we found it!' said Elle. 'I'm so glad you got the compass, Chrystal.'

'I wonder how the other groups are going,' said Ash. 'Some might be back by now.'

'Other groups might have met those guys in the ute, too,' said Laila.

'Yeah,' said Ash. Then, 'I've been thinking, you know what I should have said to him? When he told me I looked like a girl?'

'What?'

I should have said, 'Look like a dickhead, get treated like a dickhead.'

They all laughed, but Elle thought, As if you'd ever say that in a million years, Ash.

Still, he'd found two of the buckets so far, he was doing a good job.

'We'll be the last back,' she said, smiling at her team in the shining night. 'But we will have had the best adventure.'

•

She hadn't even told him her name.

'What do you mean, you're allergic to nuts? Why did you eat that then!'

She started to cry. 'I want Mummy, I want my mummy.' Her breathing became quicker, and Fred knew she had to calm down. He wished he'd listened when they'd done that first-aid course. What were the symptoms? Swollen lips or something? Rapid breathing?

'Do you feel okay?'

'My mouth feels funny.'

'Why did you eat the protein bar if you're allergic?'

'I didn't know! Mummy checks, I get Mummy to check!'

She cried more. 'I was hungry, and I can't find Nanna's house. I can't find Mummy.' She breathed raggedly between sobs. 'Where's Nanna?'

How should I know where her damn nanna is, thought Fred. But if he said that to her, she'd just cry more.

He put the stuff back in his bag. The rain was coming down. 'Come on,' he said, 'I'll take you to your nanna.'

She stopped crying so much. Her breathing was noisy, though. Like she had asthma.

'Calm down, it's all right, put your shoes on.'

She hadn't had the whole bar. She'd be okay.

'You need to help me. What's your name?'

He came close to her, her head near his. He bent to do up her shoe. He couldn't do it one handed, holding the lighter. Had to do it mostly by feel. His fingers were numb and wet. She pushed at her lips with her fingers. 'T-t . . .' she stuttered, as if it was hard to think of her own name, to get the word out. She was wheezy. She coughed. Coughed again. Fell against him, her little head heavy.

Fell over. Lay there. Had she fainted?

He stood up.

Oh, Christ.

Fred didn't think.

He ran, away from the shelter and the little girl, out into the storm and the night.

•

They continued east through steady rain for five kilometres. The track was flat, it wasn't difficult now, just uncomfortable because it was so wet. Elle wanted to do it in one go, but she knew they still had quite a few hours ahead of them, and they'd need to keep up their strength.

When she estimated they'd gone maybe three ks, she got out her water bottle. 'Let's stop for five minutes.'

They sheltered as much as they could, and Laila broke a block of chocolate into pieces and passed them around. She shivered. 'It's got colder.'

'Only when we stop,' said Elle. Ash put on his puffer jacket. Chrystal was studying the compass, turning it one way and the other.

'Are we still heading east?' said Ash, finishing off a sandwich. 'Which way's the sea, do you reckon? I keep thinking I can hear it, but it could be the wind.'

'I keep thinking I can feel a leech,' said Laila. 'But there's nothing there.'

Elle took out her pocket knife and cut rough wedges of the cake she'd made for the trip.

'Who wants some?'

She put a chunk in Laila's hands, and Ash's.

'Here, Chrystal, it's mud cake, it's yum.'

'You should try it,' said Ash, 'it's delicious.'

She didn't want it, so Elle had that piece as well. 'Do you want the cookie dough?' she asked Chrystal. 'You should have some carbs.'

A sudden gust blew through the forest, and the trees seemed to shudder. Gum leaves skipped and tumbled, somersaulting in the silver light.

'We're lucky it's a full moon,' said Laila, licking the wet mud-cake crumbs off her fingertips. 'I wonder if Johan organised it that way.'

'It wouldn't matter so much if we had the torches though,' said Elle.

'Yeah,' said Ash. 'Bloody Fred. I hope he's okay.'

'Hey, we might be the only group to ever complete a dropping without a torch or a phone,' said Elle. 'We should get an award!'

'It might give Johan ideas and he'll make everyone do it that way from now on.' Ash laughed. 'You know some parents complain about him. That he pushes kids too far.'

'Yeah,' said Elle, 'it's okay in Holland, it's such a small country that you're never far from houses. And their forests are more like oversized parks. Not like here.'

Another surge of wind.

Elle checked the watch. The light was dimmer each time. 'It's after midnight. We better keep going.'

The clouds never seemed still, they moved over the moon.

'It's a pretty wild night,' said Laila, hugging herself. 'I hope it stops raining soon.'

'Want some water, Chrystal?' Elle asked. 'You should have some. We need to keep hydrated.'

'It's still coming.'

'It's windy, that's all.'

But Chrystal held up a hand. 'My tinnitus.'

'Come on, let's keep going,' said Elle before Chrystal could say any more.

Elle looked up, the stars were appearing and disappearing. The thing was, when a storm comes in the day, you have some warning, you can see it approaching, see the type of clouds, gauge where it is. Now, at night, Elle could sense there was something going on up there, sometimes see the clouds moving, but were they those clouds that were low and full of rain? How fast were they moving? Elle didn't know.

They were in the dark.

•

He stumbled over tree roots and rocks, and whatever else was trying to trip him up. Something cut his leg, he slid and fell

145

and his hand jammed hard against a rock, ricocheting pain up to his elbow.

Fred turned, he could hear water. He flicked the lighter. The creek was flooded, rushing, swollen, he couldn't pass it, he'd have to turn around.

He ran, pushed through the bracken, the ferns. Staggering through the bush now, where was he going? Was he heading back to her? He couldn't see. He didn't even know her name.

•

They checked the compass and kept walking east. The track was rougher again now; parts were completely overgrown. Prickly plants rubbed against them, stinging and sticking. But it would be typical Johan for the hike to get more difficult as they went. Also, he would have presumed that they'd have torches. There were fewer tall trees silhouetted in the sky. It was more like scrub. 'We must be up high,' said Ash. Exposed.

'Yeah,' said Laila, 'it feels like we've climbed a lot.'

'Okay,' said Elle, 'so we keep going for about another two ks. We should get to the next bucket at one am.'

'We're supposed to be back at school by then,' said Ash.

'We'll be late, we won't be back till early morning.'

'They'll be so relieved when they see us!' said Ash. 'Imagine how –'

'That's when the storm was coming,' Chrystal interrupted him.

'What?'

'He said we'd be back at school by the time it came.'

146

'Johan? Yeah, you're right, he said early morning,' said Ash. 'When we'd all be safe back at school . . .'

Shut up, Ash! thought Elle. Don't make her more worried!

Chrystal stopped. 'We'll still be out here. When the storm comes.'

'Come on, Chrystal, the rate you're going we'll still be out here next week.'

She didn't move. Looked at them blankly, like she was trying to make sense of something.

'Chrystal, stop being paranoid! Come on!'

Chrystal didn't budge. What could Elle do? Physically push her along for the next three hours?

'Should we all close our eyes . . .' began Laila.

'No!' Elle burst out. 'We need to see! You can't just close your eyes and take deep breaths, Laila. That's not action! We need to keep going!'

Laila turned away, hurt.

'Laila, I'm sorry.'

'I'm not avoiding action,' Laila said quietly. 'I'm letting things happen.'

And she moved towards Ash.

Elle walked out the front, on her own. Now she'd upset Laila. The wind kept picking up and then subsiding. Like the weather couldn't work out what it wanted to do. 'I wish this rain would stop,' she muttered to herself. It was relentless.

She could hear Ash and Laila talking behind her. 'I wonder where those guys are now,' he said. 'Their dog was crazy, it would hunt down animals.'

Elle slowed a little so they had no choice but to reach her.

'I'm sorry, Laila. I didn't mean to diss your philosophy. I shouldn't have spoken to you like that. I was just frustrated.'

'Don't worry,' said Laila in her measured, even voice, 'it's all good.'

'Sorry, I'm just . . . stressed.'

'Doesn't matter,' Laila repeated, putting her hand on Elle's arm. 'We're all a bit stressed.'

Ash stopped suddenly. 'What was that?'

'What?'

'Did you see that? Something went across the track. It was black.'

'Could have been a kangaroo.'

'Or a wombat,' said Laila. 'A fox, some night creature.'

They scampered past, but there was nothing there. 'I swear I saw something,' said Ash.

'I believe you,' said Laila.

'I'm a bit jumpy. I think because of those guys.'

Shut up about them, thought Elle. I don't want to hear about a storm, or a pack of idiots in a ute. We need to keep going.

Ash stopped, glanced behind him.

'Come on,' said Elle, 'there's nothing there.'

On they went. Ash felt a bit embarrassed. Elle must have thought he was so easily scared – of the guys, their dogs, the fright he got just now.

'Don't you ever feel afraid at night?' he asked the others.

'Not really,' said Laila, 'it's only darkness. Except if I'm somewhere by myself, I might . . . That someone could . . . overpower me.'

Elle didn't say anything, but she knew that sense, of being alone in nature. Even in the day she felt it. She loved going for a solo run down the forest tracks or through the tea-tree scrub near the beach. It was calming – but always there was an uneasy feeling, too. That if someone came, if a man came, could she protect herself?

'Those guys could overpower me, too,' said Ash.

Ash was an understanding guy, but he didn't really understand.

Lightning flashed over the landscape, lit up the top of the hills.

'Woah, did you see that?' Ash really was jumpy.

'Mmmmmmm it can stop your heart.' Behind them, Chrystal spoke like she was scanning a website. 'Electrical current, through the body. Burns and destroys tissues . . .'

'Right,' began Ash, 'so –'

But Chrystal wasn't finished. '. . . damages the nervous system, the brain, seizures, loss of . . . consciousness.' She trailed off.

'You know a lot about lightning,' said Ash.

'It's a long way off. Remember we saw lightning before,' Elle reassured her. 'Don't worry about it, Chrystal.'

Elle was worried too, though. Johan had said the bad weather would come once they were back at school. But now they'd be back later than Johan had predicted. Hours later. It was really windy again, rain was being blown around. Their wet jackets slapped against them. They had less protection; the forest was more open up here.

Ash wanted to take Chrystal's mind off whatever she was so afraid of. All these scary lightning facts.

'How's Snoopy going? He must be getting wet.'

No response.

'Does Snoopy, like, keep you calm? Like those weighted blankets, and stuff? Maybe I need a Snoopy!' He laughed. 'Have you had it since you were a little kid?' Ash remembered his doll, Bubba, who he'd taken everywhere until she got lost, mixed up in the laundry at a hotel in Darwin.

No answer. Does she think Ash is going to make fun of her? thought Elle. Because Ash would never do that.

They walked on, trudging through the rain.

'Chrystal, please,' said Elle, 'put your jacket on.' She was dripping wet.

Chrystal stopped, leant down and slowly undid her pack. At last!

'Listen to the wind up there,' said Ash. It seemed to come in waves, huge rushes of sound and stuff falling off the trees.

'Seventeen thousand, eight hundred and ninety-seven comic strips,' said Chrystal, fiddling with the zip on her new jacket.

'Correction!' said Ash. 'You know a lot about lightning, and the *Peanuts* comics.'

'Snoopy's like your spirit animal,' said Elle, trying to make light of it. 'Like Laila's is a black cockatoo.'

'Both eyes are on the same side of his nose. In the comic.'

'I never noticed that!' said Ash.

'Started in 1950, finished in 2000.' Chrystal sighed, as if she was exhausted by recounting all those numbers. 'When Charles Schulz died.'

'So, fifty years,' said Ash.

Elle checked her watch. She could only just see it: 12:52. 'We must be nearly at the next bucket.' If we've gone the right way, she thought anxiously. The weather really was turning nasty.

The path took them down a hill, and again they seemed to be in a clearing.

'Look around here.' Elle had to speak louder over the heavy rain. The damn rain! When would it stop! They'd been in the rain for hours. Elle tried to use the light from the watch to see further than two steps. Laila and Ash did their best, peering into the forest around them.

Was that shape . . . Yes! Elle found it. Bucket number five!

'It's here,' she called. 'We've made good time!'

She knew they were only halfway there, when they should have been back at school by now. But still, they were on the right path. 'Let's get the next instruction. We're going to get there, guys!'

Ash smiled at her, rain streaming down his face.

Elle picked up the bucket. It was heavy, not empty like the others. Probably water from all the rain, she thought as she held it so it caught the moonlight.

Something was floating in watery blood.

Still, staring eyes, red flesh, ripped fur, soft ears.

Eleven

Fred turned, ran back the other way. But which way was it? Where was she?

'I'm here!' he yelled. 'Where are you? I'm here!'

They might never find her.

What kind of person was he?

To leave her.

Rain poured down, the sky lit up somewhere.

'Help,' he screamed out to the night, desperate.

Collapsed on his knees, hating the forest, the world, himself.

The wind was getting stronger, dark colours flew in the air.

Fred looked up. 'Help!'

Rain tumbled onto his face, into his eyes.

'Someone help me!'

•

Elle dropped the bucket. It almost toppled, but righted itself with the weight at its bottom.

'What was that?' asked Ash.

'Something dead. A rabbit, I think.'

Ash stepped forward, peered in. 'Oh god. The poor thing.'

'Leave it,' said Elle, 'don't touch it.'

'Who did that?' Ash whispered. 'Who would do that?'

The others didn't hear him. Wind rushed, trees groaned above them.

'Is there a note? Any instructions?' Laila asked.

Standing at arm's length, Elle put her hand into the bucket. The liquid was warm. She grimaced, felt around, and picked out a sodden piece of paper. The writing had washed away. She held it in her dripping hands, staring at it as if the words might appear like invisible ink.

'Not anymore.'

'Okay, well –'

A fork of lightning split the sky.

Ash startled.

'That one's closer,' said Elle quickly, nervously.

'We should get out of this rain for a bit,' said Laila.

Chrystal's voice came out of the darkness, counting in monotone. 'One, two, three, four . . .' Elle looked down at the poor dead rabbit. It was like a horror movie.

'What are you doing?' she asked Chrystal. Was this a version of her humming?

The counting continued.

'What's she doing!' Elle started to panic. She wanted to grab Chrystal, shake her, tell her to stop.

'Checking the time between the lightning and the thunder,' said Ash. 'So we know how close the storm is.'

•

'Hey.' Fred went to her.

She was trying to get up, staggering.

He helped her to stand.

'I fell over.'

She coughed, couldn't talk properly, couldn't cry.

Fred remembered first aid. Give them an EpiPen and call an ambulance. Great.

'You're okay,' he said. 'Can you walk?'

He picked her up in his arms. She was heavy, he gripped her little legs, her wet jeans. The rain crashed down at odd angles.

'Hold on,' he said.

Jagged light hit the trees. The wind blew wildly, in crazy circles. Almost no time between each crash and explosion of lightning and thunder.

Fred slipped, slid, fell over.

•

A clap, a boom. Chrystal dropped Snoopy. 'We need to shelter.'

A blast of wind.

Rain pelted down, around.

Wind whirled overhead, bark fell from the sky.

Suddenly, a vibrating roar.

Chrystal started to run. Instinctively, Elle threw back her outstretched arms to protect her. 'STOP!'

A crack like a gunshot.

A crash, something snapping. A wild whoosh of air.

They could feel it under their feet. A tremor in the earth.

A tree was coming down.

The shock went through them, hit the soles of their feet. Jolted them. Elle was trembling. Ash could feel that something, a branch, had scraped his face, it stung and he could sense warm blood filling the scratch. Another flash of lightning lit the clearing. The tree had crashed into the ground in front of them, its giant stump violently open, torn and twisted like ripped flesh, white bone. It had brought down other trees with it. Bits were still falling. Elle saw Ash's face, like a strobe light. The deep scratch ran down his cheek. Branches, trees swirled wildly, silver rain slid sideways. Lightning cracked and the whole gully lit up. Massive sound surrounded them. Another bolt of lightning, Elle raced towards a hollow base of a tall tree. 'In here!' she yelled above the surging storm.

Chrystal was screaming, 'No! No!'

Clutching Snoopy, Chrystal grabbed Ash's arm, pulling at him, sliding, losing her balance.

'Not here!' She screamed at them.

Ash tried to pull her in. 'Chrystal, we need shelter!' shouted Elle.

'It's right above us!' Ash yelled.

Chrystal had lost all control. 'It'll kill us! Get out!'

Now there was no time between the lightning and the thunder, they were on top of each other.

Another tree crashed somewhere. 'Chrystal!'

But Chrystal kept shrieking. 'Get OUT!'

It was Laila who did what Chrystal said, and the others followed. Chrystal led them rushing across the clearing, scrambling down the edge, slamming up against the trunk of the tree that had fallen. Leaves and branches, parts of trees flew through the air they could see when lit up by more lightning. The wind hurled everything around. Elle put her hands to her face for protection. Another crack, the sky bright, branches everywhere, the whole forest catching and falling and breaking.

A boom of thunder. Rain pounded them.

'Crouch,' Chrystal ordered them. 'Get down.'

A crackling, static sound split the air. A fuse, something buzzing. A shock, bright line of white, like wild wire, ran down the tall tree to the ground. Bark shot off, like an explosion. A huge crack split it down the centre, an artery, right to the base where they'd all been sheltering seconds before.

People had told Chrystal that lightning never strikes twice.

They were wrong.

•

He carried her.

How long did he run for? Fred had no idea. No direction, no plan, no time, only blind panic. Crashing through the dark, sharp, wet sticks, rocks, branches, in his eyes, hitting him, the forest was alive and angry. The sky flickered, like bad static. Her little arms and legs hanging limp, dangling, she was heavy, a dead weight . . .

Something lit up ahead. A car? A torch? He couldn't hear anything except the wind howling.

'Help!' He screamed out. 'Help!'

Fred raced towards it. Stumbling, staggering, 'Stop! Stop!'

A ute, lights, guns.

He fell on his knees, the little girl like an offering before him.

'What the f—'

'I need help! An ambulance.'

•

The four of them huddled together, watching as spitting steam ripped up through the tree. Elle felt a tingling, like fever, fill her body. Embers fell through the rain, sparkling the sky like fireworks. Sputtering flames, burnt leaves hissed on the wet ground around them. The inside of the tree looked red hot, like coals already. In one moment, cold and heat, wet and dry, bright and dark . . .

'My god, what was that?' said Ash. 'Did lightning strike that tree?' He realised he'd been gripping Laila's arm. He let go, took a breath. 'That was incredible.'

The tree burnt so quickly, rain was creating smoke and steam filled the air around them.

'I've never seen anything like that,' whispered Elle.

'Me neither, it was . . . so . . .' Ash tried to find the words '. . . powerful.' It felt almost supernatural, it looked like a movie.

Laila leant towards him. 'Ash, you're bleeding.'

Ash wiped his face and saw his own dark blood across his hand. 'It's okay,' he said, 'it doesn't hurt.' But as soon as he said the word 'hurt', he felt it.

'Chrystal,' said Laila, 'you knew.'

Chrystal stayed crouched, curled over, her head tucked down, as if she hadn't noticed that the lightning had stopped.

'Chrystal?' Laila placed her hand on Chrystal's back.

She was doing her robotic counting again. 'Chrystal . . .' began Elle. But Ash explained, 'Every three seconds between the lightning and the thunder is one kilometre.'

They huddled against the giant fallen tree, shaking, and each time lightning struck, they all counted; Chrystal aloud, Ash under his breath, the others silently. Six seconds, then ten seconds, twelve seconds, fifteen seconds.

Eventually the wind died down a bit, and the thunder and lightning weren't on top of each other anymore.

'We can get up now.' Elle stood. Her hips, her calves were stiff.

They gathered their stuff, some in the clearing, some near the tree.

'Ash, is your eye okay?' asked Elle.

'I don't think it's deep,' he said. 'It missed my eye.' He could feel blood running down his cheek, and warm blood in his hair, thickening it. Something must have scratched his head, too. 'It's just a bit of blood.' He wiped his sleeve across his face.

'Chrystal,' said Laila, 'how did you know what to do?'

Chrystal pulled at Snoopy's ears.

'Lightning's one of her expert subjects, remember,' said Ash.

'Mmmmmmmmm lightning strikes tall objects. Trees. Flagpoles. Fences.'

So the hollow of a tree in a clearing was the worst place. 'Sorry, guys,' said Elle. 'I didn't –'

'Thirty people die from lightning strikes in the United States each year. Hundreds of injuries. Mmmmmmmmmmmm permanent disabilities.'

'I wonder how many in Australi—'

'Approximately ten,' said Chrystal before Ash had even finished the word.

She felt for the lanyard that had been around her neck.

'I've lost the compass.'

•

Four guys, drunk, with guns, but Fred had no options right now.

'Have you got an EpiPen?'

'What?'

'Can you get me to the hospital? At Apollo Bay?'

'Christ, what's happened?'

'She's sick, she ate peanuts. She's allergic.'

The guy in the back peered into the light. Windscreen wipers rushed over the glass. 'Shit it's you, it's blind Freddy! We know this guy! What are you doing out here?'

Fred could see him now. It was Nate, an older guy from Grammar. He was in the same house as Fred. The worst.

'Nate, hi, can I get a lift? I need a hospital.'

'We're over O five, we can't stop at a hospital,' said the driver.

'Sean,' said a guy in the passenger seat, 'look at her, let them in and drive!'

'Shit,' said Nate from the back, 'I'm not getting involved in this.'

'Get in,' said the guy in the passenger seat. 'Move over, Nate.'

Fred lifted the little girl onto the seat, swung his pack from his back, then climbed in himself. Her face was puffy. She was half vomiting but nothing was coming up. She'd try to speak, but something had happened to her voice. Fred held her, steadying her. 'Don't cry,' he said, his arm around her small body. 'It'll make it worse.'

'Let me drive, Sean,' said the guy in the passenger seat. 'You're too pissed anyway.'

Sean revved the engine. Fred saw wild eyes in the rear-vision mirror.

'Sean, it's my ute.'

'We need to go,' shouted Fred. 'Hurry, please!'

'He's out of it,' said Nate. 'He won't be able to get us through the forest.'

'Sean, stop,' said the passenger-seat guy again. 'I'll drive.'

Sean revved the ute, taking off. It skidded, swerved, lights swung in all directions, it swerved again, Fred fell forward with her. The ute just missed a tree, keeled, nearly toppled.

Sean laughed. The guy in the passenger seat grabbed the wheel, pulled on the handbrake. The ute rocked.

'Get out!'

Sean lunged at the guy, trying to punch him.

'Get out of my car.'

Sean half fell out of the ute, his gun toppled out with him. The interior light came on. There was a rash on her neck. Fred sat back up with the little girl in his arms, next to Nate in the middle and another guy on the other side.

'Bloody idiot. Nearly totalled it. I only let him drive because he wouldn't stop hassling me.'

She was gasping, wheezing.

'Can we go to a hospital? I need a hospital.'

'That's where we're going,' said the driver. Sean was yelling from outside, he whacked the ute door with a stick as they took off.

It was only now that Fred could see the face of the guy next to Nate in the back seat.

'Matt.'

'Hi, Freddy.'

Matt had been in Fred's year. Nate's younger brother. Fred didn't want to see him, didn't want to see anyone from that school.

'Is she your sister?'

Fred shook his head.

'Who is she?'

'I don't know. She was in the forest.'

Matt nodded dumbly, as if this was normal and there were no more questions to ask.

The ute was moving slowly.

Her eyes rolled back, half closed. She flopped against him.

Fred leant forward. 'How long will it take? How long?'

'I'm going as fast as I can.'

'Where are we?'

No response.

'Have you got a phone?'

'No reception.'

'I want to call triple 0.'

Matt handed Fred his phone. 'There's no coverage . . .'

SOS only.

No service.

SOS only.

No service.

The four of them looked around the clearing for the compass but there was so much stuff on the ground – broken ferns, branches, bracken, it could be buried anywhere underneath the debris, it could have been burnt.

They stood in a little circle, soaked through, shivering, frightened and exhausted. 'What do we do now?' said Ash.

They needed to regroup. Elle was trying to think of the next steps before everyone abandoned hope completely. How could they get their bearings again?

'I think what we need to do,' she said slowly, 'is head downhill, and try to find a creek. If we follow a creek, we'll end up at the sea.' That was all Elle knew. End of her orienteering knowledge. Pretty hopeless, but it was all they had to go on now. Luckily, everyone agreed. No one needed to say it, but they'd given up on getting back to school, given up even trying to find a track, they just needed to get to a main road, find something they recognised. Get out of this forest.

They got going again, stumbling downhill, on a track that animals had made maybe, but it was hardly a track at all, just undergrowth, trees, uneven ground, fallen branches, so they had to grab on to whatever they could to stop from slipping and falling.

'There are heaps of creeks and rivers all the way along the coast,' said Ash. 'Kennett River, Skenes Creek, Wye River, the Erskine . . .'

'If we get down to the Great Ocean Road we can go along there,' added Laila, 'and turn off at one of the fire tracks, up to school.'

Ash was slightly ahead. 'Don't go too far,' called Elle. 'We can't lose each other.'

Rain came down steadily but they hardly noticed it anymore. The bushes, the big fronds of fern, drooped and fell heavily, the water weighing them down. To get anywhere, they had to constantly clamber over fallen trees. It was exhausting.

Laila touched Elle's arm. 'Listen.' The three girls stopped. 'Can you hear water flowing?'

Elle tilted her head, trying to block out Chrystal's humming, to distinguish between rain falling and water flowing.

Ash called from somewhere down below them. 'It's a creek!'

'Great! We can follow it and we won't be lost,' said Elle.

They reached Ash, and started to make their way downhill, alongside the creek. But it was harder to follow the creek than they thought. The banks were steep and slippery in the dark, there was no path.

The moon lit up a red bucket, tossing and bouncing on the water, they couldn't see which number, then it flew off.

'Did you see how fast that bucket was moving?' said Laila.

The bucket made Elle feel worried. As if all their plans, their buckets and directions and notes were so ineffective in the face of the storm. It had just picked up that bucket and tossed it wherever it wanted to. And the force of that lightning . . . 'How amazing was the lightning,' she said. 'I wish we'd had our phones and could have filmed it. Did you hear it fizz?'

'The tree burnt like in a bushfire,' said Laila. 'It's only a charge going through the air, but look what it can do.'

Ash peered over the creek, trying to spot the bucket. The creek was rushing, tumbling, there was too much water there, not the gentle sound of trickling over stones. He supposed the creek would lead somewhere, but he would have felt safer on a track.

They had to keep stopping and making sure they were all together. At least the rain had eased off.

Elle checked the time. 'The battery's nearly flat,' she said, peering at the tiny plastic window: 1:33. 'We should have been back at school ages ago.'

'Bloody Fred, he started this,' muttered Ash.

Elle looked back. Chrystal was struggling, clutching Snoopy, who was wet, muddy and wrecked. At this pace they'd never reach a road!

'Can you go any faster?' It was exasperating. 'Put the toy in your backpack!'

Chrystal didn't go any faster. 'Don't pressure her,' said Ash. 'Give her a break, she's limping, and she basically just saved our lives.'

Elle knew this, she also knew that if they'd stayed where she, Elle, wanted them to stay, chances were they would all have been killed . . . She couldn't stop thinking about it. It hadn't happened, but she couldn't stop imagining if it had. And if she'd just let Fred have the stupid cans, they wouldn't be in this situation. They'd be by the fire in the main hall, drinking hot chocolate with the others. And now Ash was telling her off. She needed to get their respect back, she was the leader. And Chrystal was so weak, so slow . . .

'Chrystal, come *on*!'

Just as Elle shouted, Chrystal cried out, a choking, coughing cry, and they scrambled back to her. In the moonlight, they could see that she had slipped, her ankle was twisted at a sharp angle, and a tree had stopped her from sliding further down into the swollen creek.

•

Fred gripped the back of the seat in front with one hand, and held the little girl against him. The driver's shoulders were hunched, he was peering ahead as he negotiated trees, gullies, potholes in the forest track.

'It's Fred,' said Matt.

'What?'

'He used to go to Bellarine.'

'Dale,' said the driver. He glanced at Fred in the rear-vision mirror. 'Hi.'

'We never saw you after second term,' said Matt.

Fred didn't speak. Her face was pale, her breathing like snoring.

'Did you get expelled? That was the rumour.'

'I left.'

'Yeah, we got PBRs, emails to the parents . . . It was pretty funny though. Sleeping Beauty. Yeah, funny.'

How could Matt even mention that now? That stupid stuff they did.

'Yeah this kid is really sick,' said Fred. 'She's had one of those reactions.'

The journey was scarily quick but felt like it would never end . . . something had happened to time in this forest, this night, and from somewhere came the story from long ago, of the girl who slept for a hundred years. Wake up, little girl, wake up. Fred felt her pulse on her tiny wrist. Didn't the princess in that story have something stuck in her throat? That became dislodged. Apple? Or was that another story. Could some of the protein bar be stuck in her throat? What was it about clearing airways, how do you even do that.

Twelve

'Look at your ankle.'

It was already swollen over Chrystal's water-logged runner. She winced when she touched the tip of her shoe to the steep, muddy ground. Elle knew Chrystal wouldn't be able to put any weight on that foot.

They helped her over to a bit of clearing, under some tree ferns, where Chrystal sat on a rock. Just to make things worse, the rain started again. They were wet, cold, they had hardly any food left, they had lost Fred, and the compass, and now Chrystal couldn't walk.

Elle's toes were numb. Her weatherproof slicker was no longer weatherproof. Laila's woollen top was soaked through. Her oilskin coat was too big for her, she looked like a child in adult clothes. Lost.

'I could make a splint,' said Ash. He scrabbled around and came back with a solid stick. 'Could you use this, like a crutch, to help you along?' But it was hard enough not slipping over with two uninjured legs. 'That won't work, Ash,' said Elle. Ash was so kind, when all she felt was frustration towards Chrystal.

'Thanks for trying,' she added. She handed him a paper towel from her pack. 'Your face is still bleeding.'

Elle sat down beside Chrystal on the rock. 'Someone's going to have to go on. The creek must lead to the sea, so we'd get to the Great Ocean Road eventually, if we follow the creek. Wouldn't we? It might be twenty kilometres.' She put her head in her hands. 'What else can we do?'

'Who should stay here then?' asked Ash.

Elle knew who.

'I'll stay with Chrystal, you two go on ahead.'

'How will we find you? How will anyone find you?'

'I know.' Elle took off her high-vis vest. 'Leave something, a trail.' She dug in her pack to find her pocket-knife and ripped a strip, then more strips, gripping the knife in her wet hands.

'Pity about your vest,' said Ash. 'Be careful, Elle, don't cut yourself in the dark.'

He and Laila ripped some too, until they had about twenty pieces of high-vis fabric.

'Here, you take the watch.' Elle checked the time: 1:45. Would this night ever end? She handed it to Laila. 'We'll stay here. We won't move. You'll have to send someone back for us.' Elle hated saying that. But she hadn't been patient with Chrystal, and now Chrystal was hurt and they were going to have to be rescued.

'Show me your ankle,' she ordered Chrystal.

It seemed to be swelling more by the second, all around her shoe.

'Okay, we'll go then,' said Ash tentatively.

Laila put on the watch, her fingers cold and shaking. Ash dabbed at his bleeding cheek with the wet paper towel.

'We'll get to a road as quickly as we can and send someone for you,' said Laila.

'Yep, okay,' said Elle. 'Take care.'

Ash took the last of the apples and the thermos from his pack. 'You have these.' He put them on the rock, like an offering in a temple.

'Thanks, Ash,' said Elle.

Ash hesitated. 'Right . . . Okay, you good to go, Laila?'

Chrystal and Elle sat on the rock in the steady rain and watched the two silhouettes until they blended into the darkness. Elle really hoped they'd find a road.

Having to sit made her start thinking again. Would Chrystal have fallen if Elle hadn't pressured her to go faster? Would they have been killed if they'd stayed under the tree? Her instincts had told her to shelter there. But that had been wrong. Elle looked to the sky, charcoal grey against the black, black trees – now the forest seemed filled with darkness, encircling them, filling them both up. There was nowhere for darkness to stop, to reflect like the sun did in the daytime.

'Did you just follow your instincts then?' she asked Chrystal. 'Before, with the lightning.'

'I knew.'

'What, you see things before they happen or something?' Elle didn't believe any of that kind of thing, it was rubbish.

A gust of wind, wet gum leaves danced. She picked up the apples and the thermos, put them in her pack.

'No, it's what happened to my dad.' Chrystal twisted her hair. It was hanging in pieces.

'The economist?'

'He was under a tree, and the tree got hit.'

'Oh, right. But he's okay now?'

For some reason, Chrystal laughed. 'Not okay, he's in rehab.'

'Oh, so he will be okay.'

Chrystal said nothing. 'Mmmmmmmmmmm . . .' Then she spoke in a rush. 'Lightning's five times hotter than the sun. One strike is a hundred million electrical volts.'

'Wow,' said Elle quietly, because, really, what else was there to say.

'He runs at night because he's very busy. He doesn't mind running in the rain. Once you're wet, you're wet.'

'True,' said Elle, 'like us, now.'

Chrystal ignored her, but went on. 'He was wearing head-phones. With metal in them. His heart stopped. People gave him CPR but he got damage.' Chrystal looked up directly at Elle. 'A storm's unpredictable,' she said. 'You can't always predict storm behaviour.'

Elle hated to hear that. Usually the weather forecast was accurate.

'Damage?' she said. 'What kind of damage?'

Chrystal's voice was suddenly soft, and Elle wasn't sure she heard her properly.

'Did you say rain damage?'

Rain fell.

'Mmmmmmm brain damage.' Chrystal repeated it. 'Brain damage. His heart couldn't pump blood to his brain, resulting in brain damage.'

'Chrystal, when did this happen?' Why didn't it say on the form under the 'Is there anything we should know about the person' question? Elle would've thought that your father being struck by lightning fell into that category. But then the form didn't say that Chrystal was quite odd and might not find it easy to fit in, either. Maybe if they'd said that, no one would have agreed to take her. Like a foster animal that nobody wants.

'Last year.'

'And he's still in rehab?'

'Six months rehab.'

Chrystal had been with them nearly three weeks. Was it her dad who she'd been messaging all the time? 'You've never mentioned this.'

Chrystal shrugged. 'Nobody asked me.'

What, thought Elle, I didn't say, By the way has your father been struck by lightning?

'What kind of brain damage?'

'Walking talking brain damage.'

'That must have been so frightening. For your dad.'

'He doesn't remember it. His eardrums were perforated. Now he has tinnitus, too.'

'Frightening for you as well, your whole family.'

'His sweat turned to steam and burned him.'

'Oh . . .'

'He was in a coma, like sleeping. For a long time.'

'Chrystal –'

'He might never come home. He was on the right side of the storm.'

'Well that's one good thing then.'

But Chrystal shook her head. 'That's the worst place to be. It's where it's strongest. That's where we were, too.'

'So, the right side is the wrong side,' said Elle.

'Yeah,' said Chrystal, 'that's right.' She held Snoopy close. 'Right is wrong.'

The rain had stopped.

Moonlight fell, branches snapped, an animal called, an owl maybe.

'My mom, she's not the same either.'

Poor Chrystal.

'And Daniel's at college.'

This was the longest conversation they'd ever had.

'So did you want to come on exchange, to kind of like, forget what had happened?'

'My mom said this would be good for me.'

'Right . . .'

Elle could hear the creek rushing on.

'Mmmmmm but I'm not friendly.'

What could Elle say? It was the truth.

'Well, we're getting to know you a bit on this –'

'I wanted to sleep, too.'

Elle thought of the Swedish children, giving up, silent and sleeping. 'Like, to forget about it?'

'For ever.'

'What do you mean, for ever?'

But Chrystal talked over her. 'You say it too. You say, "Forget about it."'

Do I? thought Elle.

'But you can't forget about things. The more I try to forget them, the more they happen. Like lightning.'

'Twice,' said Elle.

'I have to hold on to . . . hold on . . . not to freak out.'

'Do you mean here in the forest, or always, all the time?'

Eventually, Chrystal gave an answer, of sorts.

'My dad's in rehab,' she repeated. 'But he's gone.'

•

Dale sped up, the ute hurtling through the bush, almost out of control, rocks and branches hitting it from underneath as it bounced and bumped and skidded.

'Come on,' said Fred under his breath, panicking, 'come on.' Then, 'Where are we?' he shouted to Dale. 'Where are we now?'

'I'm going as fast as I can.' Dale turned, looked anxiously at Fred and the little girl. 'We're nearly out.'

Suddenly, a jolt, the ute stopped sharply and all of them in the back fell forward.

'What the f—' Nate began, but stopped. Another tree, its roots twisted in the headlights like writhing snakes, was blocking their path.

It was like coming across a smash, a wreck on a highway, carnage.

'Christ,' said Dale.

'Can you go around it?' said Fred frantically.

'Nate,' Dale ordered, 'get the chainsaw from the back.'

Nate got out, slammed the door. One of the dogs barked.

'How long will this take?' Fred shouted.

Dale didn't answer, got out of the car. The chainsaw roared to life in his hands. A terrifying sound.

Nate stood, looking on.

'Come on, come on,' said Fred in the ute, like a mantra.

She lifted her head. 'I think you fainted,' said Fred. 'Can you talk?'

Matt's voice, his dumb laugh, was right beside Fred, but it sounded far away.

'Yeah, blind Freddy. You didn't see the security cameras. You got stitched up, man.'

She was limp in his arms. She was cold.

•

Ash and Laila were following the creek. Ash was pleased to be alone with Laila. He watched her walk in the moonlight ahead of him. No detail, just the shape of her body. She moved so smoothly, the opposite of Chrystal. It was instinctive, wasn't it, you couldn't change the way you walked.

Now that the clouds seemed to be clearing, the supermoon, high in the sky, gave off even more light. They could see that, in the storm, trees had come down all over the place. Disturbed, opened up. Ash could smell the fresh eucalyptus. The rain had eased off.

'How about that lightning?'

'Yeah,' said Laila, 'that's the power of nature.'

'I reckon it was one of those mini tornadoes.'

When nature felt like it, it could really do what it wanted.

Every so often they stopped and tied a strip of high-vis fabric to a branch. The light on the watch said 2:10 am. A minuscule light, fading.

'We should put one about every thirty metres, do you reckon?' said Ash as he held a branch and Laila tied it on.

'Until we run out.'

'Hopefully we'll get to a fire track or something before then.'

'Is your face okay?' She came close. 'Does it hurt?'

'It's fine, I think the bleeding's almost stopped.' Ash felt his cheek, just under his eye, then the back of his head. His hair was matted, wet, warm. He dabbed at his face with the soggy paper towel. Laila took it from his hand. 'I can see where the blood is,' she said, touching his face tenderly. Ash closed his eyes, so that when she gave him back the paper towel, she had to lift his hand and place it there as if he was a blind person.

It was hardly raining now. The forest felt quiet after the wild noise, the energy of the storm. The flow of the creek was the only direction point they had, and all creeks eventually led to the sea, didn't they? If Elle was right, then hopefully they'd reach the Great Ocean Road. But when?

Together they slipped and slid, grabbing branches and the trunks of young trees to keep themselves from falling. Some of the trees had crashed into others, so were now on a permanent lean.

They came to what might have been an overgrown track that veered from the creek but in the same general direction. 'Looks like an old tramway track,' said Laila. 'The tramway tracks all come out at roads, in the old days horses pulled the trolleys with logs down from the mountains.'

'Should we follow this, then?' Ash asked. 'Not the creek?'

'Yeah, I think so.'

'But it's sort of heading inland, do you think it's going up or down?'

'I say we head this way.'

The track was more open and not so steep, but very muddy. Puddles reflected silver in the moonlight. It was hard to walk fast.

'You know they're still logging parts of the Otways.' Ash had seen old photos of loggers felling the giant trees. How would it feel, he thought, bringing down something so mighty.

'Yeah,' said Laila. 'I've been to the protests.'

'I don't know how people could chop them down.' It felt so violent to Ash, like hurting yourself. 'And back in the eighteen hundreds, they'd chop down the biggest tree and the stump became like a tourist attraction.'

'Yeah.' Laila gave a little laugh. 'Look how things have changed. Now, people from Melbourne come down and protest. But they're tourists, too. They have to use Google Maps to find it.'

Ash kind of got that. Even if they had no connection to the place, some city people needed to know that the forest was still here. Not totally destroyed. Like it was part of some fairy tale, still in people's imagination.

'It's so old,' said Laila quietly. 'Old growth forest.'

'Do you think it will heal? The parts that've been logged?'

'It might,' said Laila. 'Like in a hundred years. Or maybe a thousand.'

Such a long time. And Laila, she seemed to have a connection to the natural world that Ash wanted, too. He loved the beach, the forest, but he was always moving through it – surfing, walking, cycling – not stopping, touching the trees, breathing the air. Sometimes if he stopped, he felt more worried than calm – anxious that people didn't care enough about it, that climate change was wrecking it all.

Now and then drops of rain fell, and there was a rush of wind, but the lightning was further away. It was really cold though, a cold front must have come through, and Ash was hungry.

'Hey, do you have anything left to eat?' he asked. 'I'm starving, I left the last of my food with the others.'

'Here.' Laila undid her pack. 'I've got chocolate sultanas. Will they do?'

'Thanks.' Ash put his wet hand in the plastic bag and could feel her hand underneath, holding it.

'Laila, you're so cold.'

'It's because my scarf is wet.' She unravelled it and tied it to her backpack. She was shivering.

'Here,' said Ash, 'have my fleecy, I've got my puffer jacket. It's good down to below zero. I had it when we lived in the desert.'

'You might need it, we're so wet that it's hard to warm up.'

'No, you have it.'

Laila leant back against a tree. Did she close her eyes? Ash didn't want to stop her. Maybe it was important, she was meditating or something. She looked very small against the broad trunk of the beech. Didn't she want his polar fleece?

'It's not that I think you're weak or anything,' he said quickly. 'It's just that you're shivering. And I don't know how warm your oilskin is. I know you don't like polar fleeces, but you don't want to get hypothermia. Laila?'

Laila opened her eyes, then put the empty plastic bag back in her pack. 'That's the end of our food.'

'Well we won't run out of water,' said Ash. 'And don't worry, I reckon we'll get to a road soon. We should keep going, we shouldn't stop.'

'Those guys, in the ute,' said Laila. 'I hope they don't come back.'

'Are you okay, like are you frightened?' Was she shaking because she was scared?

'Not frightened,' said Laila.

'I hope the others are okay. And Fred . . .' Ash paused. 'I'm sorry Fred was such a dick to you.'

'It's not your fault,' said Laila. 'You're not responsible for what Fred does and says.'

'And listen, I didn't talk about you like that, didn't . . . objectify you.'

His parents had talked with him about objectifying women. He would never do that. See someone like an actual object. That you can use. Not treating them with dignity and respect. But if, say, he wanted to touch Laila, to hold her, to kiss her face, was that objectifying her? Ash hoped not. Standing here in the moonlight, everything glistening, with this girl, a girl whose voice he could listen to forever . . . Am I allowed to look at her, to want her? Am I allowed to say that? How could I ask her if she wants that?

Ash wanted to be a good man. Paul was a good man. Johan was a good man – although he was stubborn. Did girls trust guys at all anymore though? Did guys trust girls? It was hard to know what a girl wanted, and you didn't want to read the signs wrongly or you could really upset someone, and you could also be destroyed.

Everyone knew him as Ash, the nice guy, the friendly guy, the guy with two mothers who was so hip and could talk to girls. But behind this, Ash felt . . . what?

'I'm as scared of those guys as you were,' he told Laila. Maybe more scared, he thought. Like Elle had said, they were toxic. He hated men like that, hated that phrase, toxic masculinity. As if everything a male touched turned to poison. Like the Midas touch, except the opposite.

'Yeah, but you'll never be as vulnerable, like in your body,' Laila was saying. 'That someone could hurt you, that it could always happen.'

'Those guys could hit me, bash me up.'

'Yeah, but –'

'And Elle,' continued Ash, 'she's so strong. I reckon Elle could fight a guy. You know Elle can lift thirty kilos?'

Ash couldn't see Laila's face, she had turned away into the darkness; he wasn't sure that this was the right answer.

'Will we keep going now?' he said gently. 'It might warm you up?'

Laila shuddered. 'I will take the fleecy if that's okay. I am pretty cold. I'll put it on under my Driza-Bone.'

He held it out to her, like dressing a child. When she had it on, he smoothed it down. Without thinking, Ash rested his head against Laila's back.

Her breathing was like the ocean.

What was this.

Through his fleecy, she smelt like the forest, incense, warm.

They needed to move but they weren't moving.

When Laila spoke, Ash felt a vibration through her back.

'Even in the dark, the sky is lighter than the trees.'

He wanted her to keep talking, he just loved listening to her speak. Her voice was a bit husky. It was particular, he'd never met anyone with a voice like that.

Ash looked up. The trees, like black cut-outs against the charcoal sky, were taller here than in any other part of the forest. The moon was behind clouds again, making their ragged edges almost white – and yes, everything did feel lighter, bigger, swelling like the huge tides, beautiful and bright.

•

Dale had cut through one section of the trunk. It was taking too long!

'Is there another way?' Fred cried.

'Dunno,' said Matt, beside him.

Fred's fingers found the black tourmaline in his pocket. He clutched it.

She was lying across his lap. Should he sit her up? He felt her pulse. Still there.

Matt got out of the ute, and Fred was glad. He sat her up a bit. Her head fell down.

Now Nate had an axe and was hacking and chopping at the fallen branches. On the back of the ute, the dogs were barking again.

The three of them pushed and rolled bits of tree trunk to the side.

Fred was crying now, out of his mind with despair.

'Hurry!' he yelled.

Dale threw the chainsaw in the back, and jumped into the driver's seat, Nate in the front beside him. The engine roared. He shoved the gearstick. The ute lurched, revved, bashed through the gap they'd created in the fallen tree.

They were moving again. Fred couldn't see straight. The colours of the night, swirling around him, mingling with his tears. In the headlight he saw a flash of high-vis, through the trees. He saw only colours, he couldn't see anything.

Thirteen

The old track was hilly, but it ended up alongside the creek, which they followed as best they could. Still, it felt to Ash as if he and Laila weren't getting out at all, but heading deeper into the forest. They heard night animals. Drops of rain. The crack of a branch breaking, falling, landing in the wet ferns below.

They stopped to tie another ribbon on some bark hanging from a gigantic tree.

'I wonder how old they are,' said Ash. He held the bark, she tied the fabric, their fingers touched.

'The base is really old,' said Laila. 'Up the top is young, new leaves, new growth.' She turned to Ash. 'You can see time in a tree.'

She spoke in such a cool way, like a song or something, she said such interesting things.

'You really understand trees, Laila.'

She smiled. 'Remember, I live in a treehouse.'

Ash had only been to Laila's house once. It wasn't a regular treehouse, it was like one of those amazing treehouses you see in coffee-table books about treehouses.

'In the version of Cinderella we had,' Laila said suddenly, 'there was no fairy godmother, but there was a tree.'

'What kind of tree?'

'A magic tree.' She almost whispered the words.

'What, like a wishing tree?' Ash felt so un-magic, so heavy and earth-bound, beside her.

'It held the spirit of Cinderella's dead mother.'

'Woah,' said Ash, 'creepy.'

'I didn't think so,' said Laila.

'Even though you were a little kid? Just thinking about that is freaking me out a bit,' said Ash as they walked on. 'That and the spooky sounds. Can you hear the frogs?'

'I don't think those sounds are spooky,' said Laila.

'Laila, you're not scared of anything!'

'I was born in the forest. I like the dark,' said Laila. 'Dad says it's because of my name.'

'Laila?'

'It's a name given to girls born during the night.' She paused. 'What about your name? Ash.' She lingered on the shhh part of his name, which made Ash shiver.

'It's like ashes,' he said, 'but it's also the ash tree. My grandparents planted one in their garden when I was born.' He paused. 'Its leaves would be golden, now.'

'How big is that tree?'

'I haven't seen it for a while. It's probably a bit taller than me. Still a small tree, but it'll grow. My grandpa told me in some cultures the ash tree is sacred, a tree of life.'

'That's a good name, then,' said Laila, and Ash felt very alive, here, now.

They reached an old wooden bridge crossing the creek. 'Yes!' said Ash. 'A sign of civilisation! I was beginning to think this track was leading us nowhere.'

The railing of the bridge was rotting, it felt slimy. Part of it was broken, and half falling into the rushing water. 'Look,' said Ash, 'the creek's almost over the bridge in the middle. I suppose we cross here? It looks like the track might continue on the other side.'

They tied a ribbon around a broken post, and went across, jumping over the deepest part where the creek was washing over. Water swept over Ash's shoes, cold rushed into his socks and reached his toes.

They stopped at the other side for a moment.

'Did your feet just get totally wet?' he asked.

'Yeah.' Laila lifted her face, her silhouette like a pointer reading the conditions. 'But they were pretty wet anyway.' She had a turned-up nose. A ski-jump nose, people called them.

'Do you reckon the track continues here?' In the moonlight they could only see a few steps ahead. 'I feel like we're going the right way,' said Laila.

Ash lifted his face, too. He didn't know what he felt. They strode on, along the rough path.

'Do you think we're moving away from the creek?' he asked. 'I can't hear it as loudly anymore.'

'Yeah, but we keep coming back to it.'

Laila was right, the track seemed to veer away and then return to alongside the creek.

In the day everything was easy, no one ever got lost. But at night, and without phones and Google Maps, it was like they had no senses at all.

'My feet are so wet,' said Ash. 'They're squelching.'

'Mine too. I hope we don't get leeches.'

As soon as anyone mentioned leeches, Ash could feel things, cold on his ankles, his neck, up his sleeves. 'What's the time?' he asked. 'We really need to get help for the others.'

Laila stopped, peered at the watch. 'It's two forty-seven. Hopefully we'll get to a road soon.'

'Do you feel tired?' Laila asked him.

'Yeah, my legs are tired. How about you?'

'Yeah, a bit.'

'No wonder,' said Ash, 'we've been walking all night.'

The creek sound was closer, now. 'I think we're near the water again,' said Laila.

'That's good. Hey, look, it's another bridge,' said Ash as they came to some rotting wooden fencing. 'Like the one we crossed. Should we cross back again, do you reckon?'

'What's this?' Laila went closer. It was one of their high-vis ribbons.

Ash leant against the slippery, mossy railing. 'No . . .'

'It's the same bridge,' said Laila. 'We're going round in circles.'

They were back where they'd started.

Ash looked out into the forest. 'What do we do now?'

That was when he saw a face.

•

He held her in his arms. Her body was floppy, her head lolled back. They bounced over logs and rocks like there was no path at all. He could feel her ragged breathing against his cheek.

Was this like what Elle said? About the kids in Sweden. 'Don't give up,' he whispered to her. 'Don't give up.'

Never had he wanted something so much, so badly.

Fred often felt that he was on some collision course with himself. That something terrible was always about to happen. That he was living in fear of what he'd do next.

He thought it had been the stupid thing he did at school.

But no.

This was it.

•

Elle was trying to work out how much time had passed. One hour? Two hours? 'How long do you reckon we've been sitting here?'

They needed to conserve their energy, but they also needed to move, so that they'd stay warm.

They shared the last of the cookie dough. It was all they had left.

'People from school mightn't be out looking for us yet, depending on what the time is.' Elle looked at Chrystal's ankle, all swollen and at a strange angle.

'How's the ankle? Any better?'

No response.

'Worse?'

'It throbs,' said Chrystal. 'I feel hot.'

But it was cold, now. Why did Chrystal feel hot? Elle jumped up and down on the spot. She hated waiting. There was some light, though: the moon was high in the sky, and very bright. 'I hope Ash and Laila have found a proper road, told someone to come and get us.' She shivered. 'It feels as if we'll be here forever, like that story where they sleep for a hundred years and the forest grows up around them.'

'We won't be here forever,' said Chrystal. 'Unless we die here and no one finds us.'

'I wasn't being literal,' said Elle. 'I was just mucking around.'

Elle put the empty cookie-dough bag back in her pack. She thought of when she'd made it, two days before. It seemed like weeks ago now, going through the steps of the recipe, simple and clear.

Maybe it was thinking of a recipe, of straightforward steps, but Elle suddenly remembered RICE. Rest, ice, compression, elevation. They'd learnt it in PE. What to do if you had a sports injury. 'I reckon we should elevate your ankle.' Elle found a rock and rolled it over to act as a little footstool. Carefully, she lifted Chrystal's leg onto it.

Rain still fell. Every so often, bark would tumble, clattering down from a tree. Now Chrystal was shivering. What was the time? When would it get light? Elle paced around, stamped her feet. Her legs were stiff and cold. 'You need to move your arms, Chrystal,' she told her, 'keep your body as warm as you can.'

'Mmmmmmmm I didn't pack my coat.'

'I know, so Mum bought you that one, but you . . . don't like it.'

'I packed my own suitcase.'

What did that have to do with it?

'Dad was in rehab.'

'Right . . .'

Elle sat, stood, sat again.

Chrystal waved her arms listlessly. 'Mmmmmmmmm I didn't really want to go with him.'

'Your dad?'

'Fred.'

'What?'

'When he went up the hill.'

'Oh, right.' Even that felt long ago now. 'I'm glad you didn't go with him. Hey, if Fred's got back already, they might have sent a search party for us.'

'I wanted to go with him but I didn't want to go with him.'

'Yeah . . .' Although Elle wondered now whether Chrystal might have been better off with Fred. He was probably back at school, warm and dry, by now.

'I practise.'

'Practise what?' It was hard to follow Chrystal's train of thought.

'Fitting in.'

Okay, that's not really working, thought Elle.

'Mmmmmmm I thought he may have liked me.'

Fred? Did Chrystal seriously think he liked her?

'Yeah, he turned out to be a pain, didn't he,' said Elle.

Chrystal winced.

'Are you okay?' Elle asked. 'We should take your shoe off.'

'The more I try to fit in, the more I don't . . .'

'Right.' Elle knelt and held Chrystal's foot gently in her hands. She loosened the laces. 'Tell me if it hurts.'

Chrystal laughed oddly. '. . . fit in.'

Elle stopped, still holding Chrystal's foot. So even though Chrystal acted as if she had no idea that her behaviour was odd and inappropriate, she did seem to have some insight. Elle was confused. Why do people like that not just alter their behaviour? Was it simply too hard? Was Chrystal too stressed? Elle thought of those kids in Sweden – they had no control; they literally went into a coma. It made Elle wonder how much real control anyone has over the way they speak, how they act, how their body works. We think we have control, thought Elle, as she eased the shoe from Chrystal's swollen ankle, but some other part of us seems to be working in another way, a way that we're not aware of. She shook her head. A mystery.

'Mmmmmmmmmmmm he feels sad,' Chrystal was saying, stroking Snoopy.

'Huh? Snoopy?'

'Fred is sad.'

Elle hadn't thought of it that way. She thought Chrystal sometimes seemed sad, but Fred? More like angry. Still, sadness can sometimes look like anger. And the other way around, too. Chrystal seemed so indifferent; her eyes often looked vacant. But what if they weren't vacant, what if they were trying to adjust? To what she was seeing, feeling.

Elle bounced on her toes to keep her circulation going. Silver drops from the trees spattered on her coat. Help might be hours away. 'We might have to wait till morning,' she said, 'till it's light, then I could go and find someone.'

'Mmmmmm don't leave me.'

Elle sat back down next to Chrystal. 'Okay then. Don't worry, I won't.'

They listened to the after-storm sounds. The forest settling back into place. Dripping. Ticking, connecting.

'Has your tinnitus gone now?' Elle asked.

'Not gone, but not as loud.'

'Do you hear it all the time? Like is it constant?'

'Mmmmmmmmm not when I'm near the sea, or in a storm.'

'How come?'

'The sound of rain and waves blocks it.'

'What does it sound like, tinnitus?'

No response.

Then, 'Wind past my ears, the whole world rushing at me. Breathing in my ear, too close. It makes me go off balance, like I'm going to fall.' Chrystal moved her leg slightly.

'Are you right?' Elle asked.

'I hear ringing, a high pitch. And whooshing. Mmmmmmm some people hear hissing, static, screeching, roaring, pulsing, buzzing –'

Chrystal stopped her monotonal list because they'd both heard another sound. Something falling? The wind picking up? Was that a light? Help had come already! It wasn't coming from the direction that Ash and Laila had gone, where they had tied the fabric. Torchlight shone through the forest. As the beam of light swept over, Elle stood up, saw the track, the ribbons tied . . .

190

'Over here!' she shouted. 'We're over here!'

A figure broke out of the forest.

He pointed a gun at Elle.

'Don't move.'

Fourteen

They screamed out onto the road, the ute swerving wildly, nearly hitting the low fence barrier beside the rocks and crashing ocean.

'How far is the hospital?'

Nate turned in the passenger seat. 'Is she breathing?'

Fred put his hand on her chest.

'We need to do CPR,' said Nate.

'I don't know how!' screamed Fred. Because he'd never listened! *NEVER* LISTENED in any class, to anything he was supposed to.

He hugged her to him, held her with all of him, darkness and light swirled, she was his.

'Pull over,' Nate told Dale.

The ute slowed down.

'Don't stop!' shrieked Fred.

'Shut up!' yelled Nate. 'Matt, get in the front.'

Matt was silent, white faced, did what his brother said.

Matt and Nate swapped seats so Nate was in the back with Fred.

Dale took off again, the ute skidded in the gravel.

'Move her, over here.'

'She's got a pulse,' said Fred, 'I can feel it.'

Fred hated Nate, he was a bully, a thug at school, but as the ute sped along the road, Nate tilted her head, leant down and breathed into her mouth.

'Now push,' he said. 'Push her chest.'

Fred put his hand on her, her small body, and pushed.

'Harder, her chest has to rise, harder!'

He shoved Fred. 'Get out of the way.'

Nate took over, pushing down hard on her chest.

'We're nearly there,' yelled Dale from the front. 'I see the lights.' The ute sped up.

'Hold her still,' Nate ordered.

'You're going to break her,' Fred cried, kneeling on the seat beside her, trying to hold her small body so it didn't roll off as the ute went even faster. 'Don't break her bones!' It felt so brutal, so wrong.

Fred was sobbing now. 'Don't hurt her.'

Nate ignored him, his big fingers and thumb gripping her little nose, he bent and breathed again into her mouth, covering her.

He was hopeless, stupid, blind Freddy. He clutched the stone.

Help me, Fred pleaded silently. Help me.

•

Ash's heartbeat thudded through his body.

He pointed. 'What's that?'

Laila peered into the shadowy undergrowth. She took a step . . .

'It's an owl. A Powerful Owl.'

'Oh phew!' Ash was mesmerised by its staring, yellow eyes. 'Yeah, it looks powerful,' he added.

'No,' Laila said softly and he could sense that she was smiling, 'that's the type of owl. It's called a Powerful Owl.'

'Oh, well it nearly gave me a heart attack!' Ash laughed with relief. Then he felt stupid, because he did know the Powerful Owl, he'd heard of them, but they weren't owls that lived in the Kimberley.

They stood at the bridge; they could see the high-vis ribbon that they'd tied on the first time.

'Do you reckon we cross back now? Should we keep on the side of the creek we were on before? Keep heading down and stay on the one side?'

There was a rustle, and the owl swooped, picked up something from the forest floor, and flew off. Its silhouette was huge and silent.

'It's a sign,' said Laila, and Ash almost laughed, then realised she was serious. 'Let's follow the owl.'

They'd tried following paths, creeks, tried a compass, tried the buckets, tried the stars, tried intuition . . . What the hell, thought Ash, let's try an owl. Did he have any better ideas?

'Where is it now?'

'That way.' Laila pointed. 'It's guiding us.'

They left the track and headed through the bush in the direction of the owl. 'Hang on,' said Ash, 'we need to tie another bit of ribbon.'

Together they fastened another piece of fabric to a branch. 'Can you hear it now?'

'I think it's this way.'

They moved slowly through thick grasses and bushes, around ferns and trees. Wet leaves and drooping branches brushed against them. Sometimes they lost their footing in the mud and the bracken, and slid into each other. 'When I lived in the community,' said Ash, 'I used to hear an owl some nights. For ages I thought it was a dog. But it was a Barking Owl. Sometimes we saw them if we went out at night, in the lights from the troopy.'

'If you see them, there'd be a reason for it,' said Laila. 'The owl could be your spirit animal.'

'I wonder if this one will bark.'

'No, but they have a call.' She stopped again. 'Listen.'

But the owl didn't call. It was only the sounds of the forest. The creek, not far off, the wind above them, drops of water after the storm.

'I do like owls,' said Ash. 'I reckon they look like people, actually.'

'They have round eyes,' said Laila. 'Their eyes are saying look closer, look deeper.'

'Where is it now?' said Ash. 'I can't hear it at all.'

'They fly silently because their wings have such soft feathers.'

But as if in answer to Ash, they heard two notes, not like a bird call but a voice, almost human. It had an urgency, a tension to it. A low note and a high note. Like it was trying to say something.

'This way . . .'

Ash followed Laila.

He trusted her. It was like the forest was her place. Ash loved the Kimberley, but he knew it wasn't his place. He felt it when his friends took him to the gorge, the lagoon, the hills above their town. He loved it when they shared their stories and knowledge. Even little things, like where to find bush tomatoes, or which fish was best to eat. He had his own belonging that felt important, that he was grateful for, but it wasn't like theirs. It was their place; it could never truly be his. The country was part of them. They were willing to share it, but they had a sense of it that he didn't have, would never have.

It was wet, cold and dark, they were supposed to be getting help and they were basically lost, but something about being in this forest with Laila, listening out for the call of an owl, felt weirdly peaceful.

•

Elle could tell by his voice it was the guy from the ute. Sean.

'Not so brave now, are you.'

He stumbled. Light moved wildly around the trees, the sky.

He was putting a head torch on.

Bright white in their eyes, blinding them.

He marched further into the clearing. Aimed, laughed, came closer.

The torch lit up Chrystal. She was white, wet, frozen. Snoopy at her feet.

Suddenly, an explosion. Elle let out a shriek. She'd never heard a gun fired before. The boom filled the night.

'Get up.'

'She can't, she's injured.' Elle's voice came out a croaky whisper. 'We're waiting for help.'

'Well,' he smiled, 'here I am.'

He reloaded the gun. Came closer still. Elle smelt something burning.

Chrystal was humming, shaking, hands pressed hard over her ears. Her eyes were closed, gripped shut.

'Can you . . . put the gun down?' said Elle, trying to stop her voice from trembling.

He grabbed Elle by the shoulder. 'You owe me an apology.'

She could smell his breath, a sweet sick smell of Coke and alcohol. He put his fingers up to her face. To her mouth. They were rough, thick. Elle tasted something metallic.

Instinctively, she kicked out at him. He lost his footing and she ducked out of his hold. He was slipping in the mud and the leaves. He swore, still holding the gun. A beam of light arced through the sky. The gun went off again, a terrifying echo through the whole forest.

Elle grabbed Chrystal's arm. Chrystal yelped in pain as Elle dragged her, hopping and limping out of the clearing and into the dark of the trees.

'Shhh, shhh. Please, Chrystal, we can't run, we'll have to hide.' They crouched down, tried to go a bit further, slid down the muddy bank towards the creek edge.

'He's coming!' whispered Chrystal. They could hear him swearing and stumbling about.

'He's slow,' whispered Elle. 'He's drunk.'

Cold water took their breath away. Their feet, their legs were in the creek.

Where was he? The light moved around, then seemed to fade off, disappear.

Elle edged up and looked over the bank. 'I think he's gone.'

'He might come back.'

Elle slid back down. 'Let's wait till we're sure then go back to our spot. Someone has to come soon.'

They crouched forever on the creek bank, freezing water rushing over their shoes. Elle's ears were ringing from that gunshot.

'It's okay, Chrystal,' said Elle after a while, 'let's go back now. Here, I'll help you, I know it hurts.'

They scrabbled back up the bank, making their way towards their waiting spot.

'What did he want?'

'I don't know, to scare us?'

Chrystal hopped, leaning heavily on Elle. Elle could have outrun that guy easily. But Chrystal couldn't walk, clearly it hurt her to even move. And he had a gun.

A beam of light . . .

Then darkness again.

Elle and Chrystal scrambled back down to the creek bank. Commando crawled through the cold mud, dragging their legs behind them. Elle pulled Chrystal out of the light of his head torch. 'Don't move,' she whispered.

Silence. Where was he? The light was casting behind them.

Phew. Was he heading away?

A splash . . .

It felt close.

A tiny sound . . .

Oh no . . .

Chrystal, Elle prayed, please, don't.

'Mmmmmmmmmmmmmmmmm . . .'

•

Laila and Ash went further into the forest, following the owl's call and its whispery wings. 'Keep up,' she told Ash. Then, 'I keep stumbling, I need to hold your arm.'

Ash felt her hand, her fingers pressing against his arm through his jacket.

Automatically, he flexed his bicep.

'The moon might be setting, it feels like it's getting darker.'

The ground was steeper, too. They were quiet, focusing on keeping their balance. Then they heard it again. The two notes. 'This way,' said Laila. They were heading away from the creek. The forest was denser. They were getting even more lost, he could feel it. They stopped, listened. Should they be doing this? Ash almost felt in a trance.

'Can you feel a connection through my arm, my hand?' Laila asked.

'Um, no.' She said some funny things.

'You should feel it. It's the chakras.'

'Oh, maybe there's something wrong with me then. What should it feel like?' Ash guided her around a boulder.

'Like swirling wheels of energy.'

'Right.'

She grabbed a branch to steady herself.

'Oh, maybe I can feel it. Is it sort of like . . . pressure?'

'It's because I've got an open-heart chakra.' Laila paused. 'I have an open heart.'

'Can you feel my energy through my arm?' asked Ash.

Laila didn't answer, which made Ash uneasy. 'Lol,' he said, 'maybe my heart chakra's blocked.'

'That's a thing,' said Laila. 'It can be blocked.'

'How would I know, if I had a blocked heart chakra?' It sounded like a blocked artery or something.

'Do you think it's blocked?' Laila asked him.

'I don't know.' He laughed softly. She let go, and they continued on.

Ash couldn't explain it, but something in him felt that might be true. Sometimes he did feel a bit . . . blocked. Like to himself. He didn't totally feel that he knew who he was. He adjusted his senses to the situation he was in. Ash's parents seemed to know who they were. It was like their place in the world was doing good deeds. They were such good people . . . Sometimes he felt the urge to do something his parents wouldn't like, but he didn't even know what that was. And they'd probably understand, even if he did.

The owl called again.

They stopped to tie another piece of fabric. 'Let's spread them out a bit more,' said Laila, 'or we'll run out.'

'Yeah I hope we get somewhere, soon.' Ash pictured Elle and Chrystal, back there, waiting for help.

'So do you know all this stuff because of your dad?' he asked Laila when they'd tied the fabric. 'About the chakras and energy?'

'I suppose,' said Laila.

'It must be great having a dad like that. Everyone loves him.'

'Yeah.'

'And he wrote that mind body spirit book. Doesn't he have like a million followers on Instagram?'

The owl called again. 'It's really guiding us,' said Laila, excitement in her voice. 'This way.'

They went up and over a leaning tree fern.

'Does your dad teach you new yoga moves at home?' Ash asked.

'Not really, he travels a lot.'

'Even in lockdown?'

They heard the owl again. 'It's actually like it's calling to us,' said Ash.

'It is.'

They continued on, to the heart of the forest.

'Your dad must be so . . . enlightened.'

As they stood listening out for the owl again, 'You know what?' Laila said suddenly. 'He's not that great at helping us.'

'Who do you mean?'

'His family, his daughters. Me.' She paused. 'When I broke up with Joe, this guy I was seeing –'

'Yeah I know Joe,' said Ash, 'in Year Ten.'

'– Dad was hopeless at giving me any advice.'

'But he's a guru. People must ask him for advice all the time?'

201

'Yeah.' Laila stopped. 'It was like he didn't want to know me as soon as I started seeing Joe.'

'Right,' said Ash, gently guiding Laila on, 'so your dad didn't like him.'

'It wasn't really that,' said Laila. She walked lightly over the bark, strewn branches, uneven forest ground. 'He seemed to like Joe, it was more that Dad didn't like me, when I was dating Joe.'

What? Ash felt out of his depth. 'Did he like you again once you'd broken up?'

'I don't know, things just . . . changed. But like I said, he was totally hopeless at giving me advice. He didn't even want to talk about it.'

'So . . . is he not who he says he is?'

'No, that is a part of him.' Laila took Ash's arm again. The mud was so slippery! 'The guru thing is more what he wants to be, how he wants to be seen.'

Like me, thought Ash. Like Fred. Like everyone, maybe.

Ash had never heard Laila talk about her dad, except to mention him in Junior Guru class, and nod and smile when people said how great he was. Was it the darkness now, being alone in the forest with Ash, that gave her the permission, the strength, to be more honest?

'That's weird, isn't it. Because he's like the authority on wellbeing and stuff.'

'With the public.'

They tied another ribbon.

'How many are left?'

'Three more.' Ash didn't know what they'd do when they ran out.

'Listen, I love him.' Laila for once seemed a bit rattled, but she had some kind of momentum within her and couldn't stop now. 'I mean he's healed so many people, even people who've had terrible injuries, like broken their back. And Oprah chose his book for her book club. He's a great dad. But he doesn't . . . he can't help us in the way he can help strangers.' She paused. 'At home, Mum just does what he says.'

They came to the shadowy form of an enormous tree. 'Hang on, where's the owl?' said Ash.

Silence.

'I think we've lost it. Laila, I'm not sure we should have followed it. The forest is so thick here. It's really hard to get through.'

They stood side by side in the dark.

'What's the time?' Ash asked. 'We're taking forever.'

Laila pushed the little button on the side of Elle's watch.

A last bit of weak light: 3:57.

Then nothing.

'I think the battery's flat,' said Ash.

Laila took his hand, and something drummed in his body. She spoke quietly into the night. 'Then we'll use our other senses.'

•

A voice from above them, at the top of the bank.

'I see you,' he half sang.

He was playing with them.

Hunting them.

Elle grabbed Chrystal's arm. He fired another shot, just in front of them. It ricocheted, splattered into the black water. Elle heard a sharp click as he reloaded, then suddenly he was sliding down towards them, fighting and grappling, slipping on the muddy bank. Light went everywhere, crazed. They were half in the creek. He was holding Elle. Gripping her. She was thrashing, pushing against him, couldn't see, losing, falling.

A shot rang out.

The struggle stopped.

Chrystal was on the bank, the gun in her hands.

'Get away . . .' she said.

He stood up, stumbling, off balance. 'Give me –'

'. . . or I'll shoot you.' Chrystal steadied herself against a tree.

Elle scrambled from the water and gripped the bank on her hands and knees.

'Go that way, across the creek,' Chrystal shouted into the dark. 'Go back to your buddies.'

'Give that back, you mad –'

Chrystal raised the gun. Elle gasped.

The guy lumbered up towards Chrystal, panting.

In the wild arc of light, Elle saw Chrystal take aim.

'Chrystal, no!'

Time stopped. The torch shone on Chrystal's face, her soaking clothes, the gun about to fire.

'Don't come any further.'

He kept coming.

Chrystal fired again. Her arm flew back, her shoulder jolted. Elle jumped, nearly slid back down. The torchlight fell.

'Quick, let's go.'

They hobbled, limping – cut by sticks and branches, water-logged, mud-soaked.

They stopped against a tree. Elle fell against Chrystal, who almost toppled over.

'Chrystal,' said Elle, panting, 'you shot him.'

•

Ash and Laila had to go slowly through the watery forest. They'd lost the owl, but it had led them to this creek – black and rushing, flooding over the ground. It was impossible to walk quickly through mud. Mud, everywhere. Wet, smelling of the earth.

'Do you still sense that we're going the right way?' Ash asked. 'To the ocean, the road?' Something thorny kept scratching him. Blackberries? 'Now the other side looks easier again, more open. Always the side we're not on.'

Laila peered across the creek. 'It's hard to see how open it is. Anyway, we can't cross anywhere here, the creek's too high. We need to find another bridge.'

'I don't know how far we can go on this side, though.' Sharp, sticky reeds caught on their clothes, cut their hands.

But Laila was right, the creek was deep and rushing, branches tumbled down with it, flowing fast. As if all the energy of the storm had entered it.

They pushed aside the reeds, holding them back for each other. 'This stuff hurts,' said Ash. 'Is it cutting your hands?'

'Yeah,' said Laila. 'But it's the only thing to hold on to.' She sighed. 'We're not really getting anywhere.'

It was exhausting, they were exhausted. 'I reckon if we find somewhere we could cross over again, we should try that,' said Ash.

'Okay,' said Laila, 'we can try . . .'

'We need to get help.'

'I hope they're okay. I hope the stones will protect them. Elle and Chrystal.'

'I hope Fred's okay, too,' said Ash, 'wherever he is.'

They slipped and slid and struggled, and a bit further on they came to a fallen tree, high across the creek.

'Reckon we can get across?' Ash asked.

'I don't know,' said Laila.

'I'll go first,' said Ash. Now she'd see that he was brave, not like when he'd been spooked by sounds, or stood shaking in the clearing, scared of the dog and that awful Sean guy. Ash went forward and straddled the tree trunk, it was mossy and wet. He edged along like a kid on the end of a seesaw. 'It's okay,' he said, 'come on.'

He looked back to see Laila's silhouette moving now along the tree. It was slippery, hard to grip, but Ash knew Laila had strong hands from playing the double bass. Every time he turned around, it upset his balance, but he needed to see that she was okay, that she was still behind him. He had to grip the tree trunk with his legs, like riding a horse bareback, silver-black water gushing under him. Moss came away in his hands.

'Laila, are you there?' he called over the rushing water. 'Are you still behind me?' The creek was loud out here in the middle.

Shit! Was that a gunshot? Ash turned, swivelled his body.

And tumbled sideways.

His back hit the stones, a cold, sharp hurt. Ash gulped, his mouth suddenly full of freezing, rushing water, he tried to hold on to something, but the creek took him and his body hit against branches, rocks, he was being dragged down the creek, away from Laila.

He grabbed a branch that was wedged somehow. Icy water covered him. He couldn't stand, his shoes slipped against the stones at the bottom.

'Hold on!' Laila yelled from somewhere.

The branch started to move . . . his weight was pulling on it . . .

Laila was on the bank, she moved down to the water, tossed him her long scarf.

Ash grabbed it, Laila held it, braced herself against a tree, and he dragged himself up the bank.

His wet hair fell around him, heavy like sheep's wool.

He coughed, choked, gasped for breath.

'You're okay,' said Laila, crouching down beside him.

Ash fell back amongst the ferns and mud of the forest floor.

'That . . .' he said breathlessly, 'was a great idea of mine.'

She smiled, leant over him, like he'd been asleep, hidden here in the depths of the forest, and only she could wake him.

•

'I don't think I shot him,' said Chrystal as they limped through the darkness. 'He's following us. See the torchlight? He wants his gun.'

A beam of light was moving fast, then slow, in and out of the undergrowth, down and then up again.

Chrystal was hobbling, with each movement she made little outward breaths.

'You can't walk. He'll catch us.' Elle crouched down. 'Get on my back.'

Chrystal was small but surprisingly heavy, like she had no muscle tone at all to cling to Elle. And everything was wet, which made her heavier still. The gun banged against Elle's leg as she moved. They'd left their packs back in the clearing, so would have to do without them now.

'You could have killed him. What if he dies? You'd go to prison.'

'He could have killed you,' said Chrystal. Chrystal avoided touching, but she had to hold Elle, now, had to put her arms around her neck.

When she felt Chrystal's small hands, Elle sensed something strange in her body; not an emotion, but a pressure, a heat, something caving in. And suddenly she had no control, as warm tears – relief, fear, exhaustion – ran down her face.

Chrystal didn't see them. 'I fired at his feet,' she said. 'It was hard to see, his torch was blinding me.'

'Where is he now?' Elle looked behind them. Turned in a full circle. No light. She swallowed. 'Do you think he's switched his torch off?'

No answer, but Elle could feel Chrystal's body tense.

Elle pushed on as quickly as she could, but the ground was slippery, uneven, and she had to scramble through the ferns, get through this dense bush somehow, not fall or trip.

'Do you think we've lost him?'

'I can't see any light.'

Elle couldn't stop shaking. She tasted salt on her lips. Her whole body was juddering, making Chrystal shake too. 'I think we're in shock,' Elle said. 'We've had a big shock . . .' She couldn't stop the tears. What was this terrible, terrible night? You're the leader, she said to herself, pressing on. Stop crying!

'I think he's gone,' said Chrystal.

'But wouldn't he still want the gun?' Elle desperately wanted to stop, to rest, but she couldn't do that. What if he was still close by? Her legs felt like they might give way, but she kept going.

Chrystal had to slide off so they could both climb over a fallen tree.

'Just give me a sec.' Elle leant over, resting her hands on the tree trunk. She sniffed, got a grip. 'Where did you learn to shoot like that?'

'Hunting deer with my dad.'

Hunting. It was so foreign to Elle. 'What, kids hunt deer? In Wisconsin?'

'Anyone can use a gun. I'm allowed to.'

'Should we leave the gun here? It's hard to carry.'

Chrystal said nothing, so the gun came with them. Awkwardly, she got back onto Elle, and Elle struggled on with her silent cargo. Maybe they'd need it again. But where were they even going, now?

'I can't hear the creek,' said Elle. 'I think we just head downhill.'

But downhill went down and then it went up again. Sometimes Elle was almost crawling, it was so uneven and steep in places, and the ground was rocky and slippery one minute and then knee-deep in muddy bracken and branches the next. This was hopeless. Her back ached from piggybacking Chrystal. She had prickles or nettles or something, stinging her hands.

'Should we stop and wait for it to get light?'

No response.

Then, 'Like you said, he might want his gun.'

'Yeah, we should keep going then.' But they were so slow! In this mud, with Chrystal on her back, they'd be doing about one k an hour at the most.

'They've probably sent out a search party. Johan would have told my parents that we haven't got back.'

But if people were following the high-vis ribbons, they'd get to the clearing and find it empty.

Elle stumbled on the uneven slope, went over on her ankle, the one she'd rolled before. It was always a weakness. There it goes, she registered, but pain had become distant, she could disconnect, like she had with her knee pain, and she kept on. Eventually it became too much. 'I need to stop for a minute.' She slid Chrystal off her back and stretched out, pulling back her shoulders. Elle bent down and felt the little bump of the tendon where the old ankle injury was. She shouldn't complain, this was nothing, Chrystal's injury was so much worse. Chrystal had dropped the gun to the ground.

Elle picked it up. It was heavier than she'd imagined. The wood was cold and smooth.

'Mmmmmmmmmm he would have called out if I'd shot him,' said Chrystal, and Elle wondered if she was trying to reassure herself, or both of them.

'Yeah, hopefully you missed him.'

'I fired at his feet,' Chrystal said again.

Elle had never held a gun, she wasn't a country kid who'd been rabbiting or shooting with an air rifle. She wasn't from Wisconsin where a kid could fire a gun, where it was allowed by the law. She was a third culture kid, a kid who belonged everywhere and nowhere. And not here, now. No one was coming to help them. They were on their own. She'd have to walk out of here, with Chrystal on her back if she had to.

'Can you try to walk for a bit?'

Chrystal couldn't. 'The pain's bad,' she said.

'Like how bad?'

'Mmmmmmmmmm like I might faint.'

'Okay.' Elle crouched down. 'Up you get.'

They dragged themselves on.

'That gunshot is ringing in my ear,' said Elle. 'Like tinnitus.'

They reached another creek, or maybe it was the same creek, who knew.

'Let's stick with this one,' said Elle.

Elle's back, her neck, legs, her ankle all hurt, but she followed that creek. It became rockier, steeper. They could hear rushing, feel a tremor.

'Is that a truck?' said Elle. 'The ute?' She looked around for lights. 'Oh god, is he here?'

They stopped, listened. Chrystal was against Elle, really touching her, gripping her shoulders, the gun hard against Elle's back, still.

Fifteen

'You're as strong as Elle, or stronger.' Ash coughed, shook his head like a wet dog as they slipped and slid their way downhill. He felt so heavy, as if his whole body was full of water.

'It's the yoga,' said Laila. 'It's a form of strength training.' She squeezed the water from her scarf and tied it to her pack. 'People don't always see it like that.'

'I s'pose not.' Ash took off his sodden jacket. 'Where did that gunshot come from?'

'It'd be those guys in the ute.' Ash was aware of Laila's hand in his again. He felt all of her hand, her skin, her knuckles, muscles, its warmth. He felt like a night animal, turning up all his senses, aware of everything around him.

'Sorry I said we should cross the creek where we did.'

'Don't worry about it,' said Laila. 'It is actually easier on this side of the creek, so it might have been the right thing to do. And we'd lost our owl.' She paused. 'Except now you're freezing.'

'How do you know if an animal is your spirit animal?' Ash asked her. 'Do you always have to be given it by someone?'

'Not always,' said Laila, 'sometimes it'll present itself to you. Like black cockatoos, I always see them before something important happens.'

Right. Ash's friends in the community had spirit animals, too.

They struggled down, down, down. 'I reckon we're heading to sea level,' said Ash.

'My dad sends people on a quest to find their own spirit animal,' said Laila.

'How do they do that?' Ash asked. 'By meditating and stuff?'

'Yeah, and before the pandemic, by going on long hikes in remote places. There's also spirits in the trees. Dad says that people used to leave offerings for them, in the forest.'

They walked on, Ash tried to pick up the pace a bit, despite being freezing and dripping wet, thinking again of Elle and Chrystal.

'Do you want your fleecy?'

Ash shook his head, wringing out his jacket. 'It's okay.'

'So do you see your father much?' Laila asked him.

'Paul? Yeah,' said Ash, grabbing a branch to steady himself, 'but he's a friend, like an uncle or something.'

'What do you call him?'

'Paul. His name. He doesn't make decisions in my life, or give me advice unless I ask for it. I don't really see him as a dad.'

The creek was widening. 'This way,' said Ash. 'It's so muddy, let's get away from the edge.' He led her towards more solid ground.

'Did you want a dad?' Laila asked suddenly.

That was a hard question to answer. 'Well, I used to worry sometimes that there was no one to teach me what a man is.'

Laila stopped, let go of his hand. 'Is that what a dad's supposed to do?'

Ash laughed. 'I dunno. But now I don't think I need a male parent to turn me into a man. I just need to become who I am. Myself. Like, I don't know, a human.'

'Yeah,' said Laila. 'A human.'

She laughed, a deep laugh for a girl.

There was no one he talked with like this. He wanted to hurry, but he also wanted to focus on what Laila was asking him. It felt important, more important than how fast they could go. Or the fact that he was shivering.

'My parents have got all these values, right. They work hard, they're patient, they love each other, they love me. I don't know if that's masculine or feminine. They're just like, good people.' Ash pictured them, in the community, at home, his open, funny, happy home. Did they know he was lost, now? Ash wondered if Johan had told them.

'Sometimes I feel more connected to nature than to humans,' said Laila.

'Yeah, you seem very connected to nature,' said Ash, hoping that was the right thing to say.

Another shot rang out somewhere. They stopped still.

'I hate those gunshots.' Ash shivered. 'Are you allowed to shoot roos in the actual forest?'

'It didn't sound that close,' said Laila. 'I don't think they're nearby.' But it had given them a fright, and they sped up. The

215

creek broadened out, there were more rocks now, too, the landscape was changing again.

A large dark shape loomed before them.

'Look,' said Ash, 'it's a cave. Let's stop here for a sec, we can go in.'

'What do you reckon the time is?' he asked as they edged across wet rocks to the mouth of the cave. 'It must be almost morning? Let's wait here, just for a few minutes, in case those guys and their guns are closer than we think.'

Laila didn't answer him, because once they entered the cave, all sound fell away.

And there, along the cave wall, were tiny buds of light.

Ash took a breath –

'Glow worms,' whispered Laila.

A wall of flickering stars.

'That's incredible,' Ash whispered.

They stood, hands touching, Ash's hair dripping down. The glow worms twinkled like small, golden fairy lights. Ash smiled in the dark, almost laughed or cried, it was so beautiful. He felt the need to be silent. He almost forgot that they were lost, that they'd left Elle and Chrystal back there, that they were supposed to be getting help, that his clothes were soaking wet, that Chrystal was hurt, that Fred was god-knows-where.

'Have you ever seen them before? Laila?'

'Not this many. Not like this.'

'In a cave?'

'No, in the forest near our place. Dad's taken me there.'

They watched the lights. Ash couldn't take his eyes off them. 'It's magic,' he said quietly.

Laila's voice seemed to come out of the cave.

'Sometimes I want my dad to fail.'

Ash was surprised. 'What? Oh. But . . . he's so famous. Successful. I thought you were proud of him?'

'I think he needs to be successful to cure something in him.'

Wow, thought Ash. Here's Laila, who seems so at peace with herself, with the world, saying something like this. It was quite a big thing to admit, that you actually wanted your parent to fail . . . But Laila wasn't a bad person. She was just a person. Ash's teacher had said to him at the end of last year, 'You are what a good person looks like.' The teacher had meant it in the right way, but it haunted him. Was he really a good person, or did he just look like one? It was hard because his parents, all they did were good things, there was almost no room for anything else. Did *they* ever feel angry? Jealous? Let down?

'Sometimes,' said Ash, unaware of what he was about to say, 'I don't know what I want. I only know what others want from me.'

Laila turned to him in the soft glow of the cave.

'What do you want?'

He knew what he wanted. He wanted Laila. This felt like the only part of Ash that was true.

She bent, picked up a stone from the cave's floor, rubbed it between her fingers.

Ash touched her shoulders, her hair.

He felt suddenly confused, as if he was somehow inside the night.

He never wanted to leave.

A thought came to him. Are we still lost, or are we hiding?

Tiny lights glowed around them. Laila held the stone between her hands, opened her fingers. 'The whole forest is magic,' she whispered. 'Can't you feel it?'

•

Elle clambered up the rock.

It wasn't an engine they'd heard.

'It's falls!' Elle cried with relief, sliding Chrystal off her back again.

In front of them the rocks fell away into a ravine, a sheer rock face, with water hurtling down. It was foaming, tumbling, sending up mist in tiny droplets. It spilled over fallen boulders, broken trees. The water in the falls looked slow motion if you tried to follow it with your eyes. When you refocused, you saw it as fast-falling.

The water was white, and Elle realised they could see a bit more than before. The sky was lightening.

'Okay.' She snapped into action. 'We need to find a way down.'

The only way was to slide down the rocks beside the falls.

'You'll have to slide on your bum,' Elle told Chrystal. 'Let me take the gun.' Elle gripped it with one hand as they slid down the first bit of rock face. Chrystal cried out, landing on her ankle.

'Are you okay?'

Clearly she wasn't, that would have really, really hurt, but what could Elle do? They had to get to the bottom.

They reached an even bigger, steeper boulder.

Chrystal gripped Snoopy.

'Put Snoopy in your jacket,' Elle told her, 'you'll need both hands.'

Chrystal shoved Snoopy in the pocket of her jacket.

'I'll go first, then I can catch you.'

Elle slid down, careful not to land on *her* bad ankle.

She stood at the base. 'Okay, you go now.'

'I can't get down.'

'Just slide, let go, I'll catch you. Let yourself slide.'

Chrystal went to, but she froze, gripping the rock beside her.

'Come on, let me help you.'

Elle reached up with her arms, as far as she could. 'Chrystal, you've been so brave.' She tried to hoist herself further, closer to Chrystal at the top of the rock. 'I'll catch you before your ankle hits the ground.

'Trust me,' said Elle, the water rushing so close to them. 'Hold my hand.'

Chrystal let go one hand, grabbed at her face, she had nothing to hold.

'You helped me, Chrystal, let me help –'

She let go, slid and slammed into Elle.

'– you,' said Elle, as they both tumbled awkwardly to the base, and watched as Snoopy and the gun fell down, down, down into the misty darkness.

•

Time meant nothing now. The cave, the whole forest, belonged to Ash and Laila. The space around them fell away, they were somewhere else entirely. Ash didn't even feel cold. There was no sound.

They became part of the darkness; the cave, with its twinkling lights, was taking them in, absorbing them. Ash was filled with a feeling that he had reached something, some height or goal, even though he was totally lost, they had no food or water, and they had failed at their task. There was energy, somewhere.

Her voice, the warmth of her came closer . . .

Did she say his name?

Ash, the remains after something is burnt. But he was rebuilding, from scratch . . .

Laila, daughter of the night.

Laila lifted her arms, breathed in.

Drops of water fell from Ash, lit up, tumbled off Laila's eyelashes, from the tip of her nose, as her face touched his.

And it was as if Ash lost all senses, all feeling of his body's boundaries. Melting into the cave, the forest, the darkness of nature.

She was so dreamy and vague.

'Do you want this, Laila? Is this what you want?'

She didn't say anything, just kissed him again.

Sixteen

Sliding, falling, slow-motion moving, Elle and Chrystal finally reached the bottom of the falls.

They sat for a few minutes to recover on a flat, cold rock.

'Do you want to look for Snoopy?' Elle asked, rubbing the swelling on her ankle.

But it was impossible and they both knew it. Snoopy was gone.

Misty water rose up, coating them like dust. Elle leant her head back. She was finding it hard to think straight. Tall tree ferns lined the gully where they sat. They looked like fountains. Silhouettes of green. Nothing seemed to be in focus, or was Elle not seeing properly? The myrtle beech with its tiny, serrated leaves was almost delicate in the greyish light. Elle rubbed her eyes. And when she drew her hands away, for a moment she saw the forest differently. Not as harsh, rough, unyielding, but more like the European forests she knew – when you got really deep into the quiet of the forest, the only sound the fall of water, perhaps it *was* a softer place. Down here, there was maidenhair fern, moss, lichen. Unusually for Elle, she had an urge to lie down, rest her head on the spongy green moss, go to sleep, and wake up later when it would be daylight. Give in to this forest. Succumb. Like those kids in Stockholm. *Uppgivenhetssyndrom.*

But she couldn't do that. Elle shook her head. She wasn't sure how much longer she could carry Chrystal, actually how much longer she could go on. Still, she turned to Chrystal who seemed to be in a trance of her own. 'You better get on my back again.'

It was all downhill, but Elle had to stop herself from constantly slipping forward with Chrystal on her back.

'You're limping,' said Chrystal.

'It's fine.'

The sky was definitely not as dark. 'It must be nearly morning,' said Elle. 'If the others got to a road, they're probably back at school by now.'

That guy would never get his gun back, it was smashed and broken, submerged somewhere at the bottom of the waterfall. With poor Snoopy.

They struggled on. Everything was dripping – the forest, everything they touched, and themselves, as well.

'Chrystal, I'm sorry about Snoopy. I know how much –'

Chrystal's body tensed again, and Elle could feel a little pulse, a gulping noise, like the speech of a deaf person. Was Chrystal crying?

'Could you get another one?' she asked, as if Chrystal was a preschooler who'd lost a favourite teddy.

Chrystal didn't answer, and Elle wasn't stupid, she knew that there would never be another Snoopy.

'Sorry,' said Elle as she tried to avoid another branch before it hit them both in the face. Vines grew up and along the mossy trunks, wrapping around branches, shiny leaves hanging like a fringe.

'Mmmmmmm I have a fear of falling,' said Chrystal.

'Don't worry, I've got you.'

'I have many fears.'

'Yeah, most people do. You were pretty scared coming down those falls. But anyone would be afraid of that.'

What was Elle afraid of? Not of falling. Or was she? Falling, failing, almost the same.

'About Snoopy, we could come back here in the day? Have a look for him . . .'

The weight of Chrystal's head rested against Elle's neck, like a baby falling asleep. Elle felt Chrystal's humming, her voice.

'Mmmmmmmmmm sometimes I don't speak –'

'Right,' said Elle, 'I know.'

'– because things are unspeakable.'

And it struck Elle that maybe they were both trying to hold everything in, hold it all together.

Chrystal lifted her head from Elle's shoulder, shook it to one side as if she was trying to get water out of her ear.

'Is it your tinnitus again?' asked Elle.

'Listen,' said Chrystal. 'I think I hear the ocean.'

Elle picked up her pace, the track became less steep. It opened up, it was wide enough for a car. Now the ground was gravel, less rocky. The forest was giving way to farmland. Elle's shoulders were killing her, but she didn't care. She marched on. 'Can you still hear it, Chrystal? The ocean? I can't hear it at all. It's not just your tinnitus?'

Elle somehow found the strength to keep going, even to walk faster.

The land unfolded, and there before them was the Great Ocean Road.

•

As soon as they'd reached the hospital, she'd been taken from Fred. All he'd managed to say was, 'Anaphylactic. Nuts.'

Since then, he'd been sitting for hours in the emergency room. He'd been holding her so tightly that now his body ached, his hands, his arms felt empty.

He'd given a nurse the details of what he knew. She said they thought she was a child who had been reported missing the afternoon before.

He found out her name was Tessa. Tessa Lake.

The little shoes, pink. Rose Madder Lake. Like the colour of the sky, now, through the window of the emergency room.

The nurse had told him to wait because the police might need to speak with him. Where were the damn police then? He'd been waiting for ages.

Did these people think he'd kidnapped her or something? Think the worst of him. Fred would need to explain himself. 'We were on a hike,' he'd say, 'for school, I found her on the hike . . .' How the hell could he describe what happened.

After a while, a woman had arrived. She looked just like Tessa Lake. Same eyes, same shaped face. Pink jumper. They really liked pink. She ran to Fred and hugged him.

'Thank you. Oh, thank you.'

Fred pulled away, embarrassed. 'She ate a protein bar, I didn't know.'

'I'm just glad you found her.'

'We were hiking, she came up to me . . .'

The people at the hospital told him that he'd done so well to get Tessa here. They said nice things to him, but to Fred it felt like distant adult praise. It didn't touch him. 'Thank you,' he said politely to Tessa's mother, who went on and on about it.

Would Fred ever tell anyone? That he had left her, Tessa, just for those few moments before he'd turned around? What would have happened if he hadn't got to the creek? That was too full to cross, and made him stop. Would he have gone back? A split-second decision that would change her life, his life, this woman in the pink jumper's life.

There must be something deeply wrong with him. Something cold and hard inside him.

Someone gave him a blanket and then a cup of tea and a biscuit, as if he was an old man. They told him that Tessa had the medication now, and she was likely to make a full recovery. Apparently she'd been dropped at school by her mum that morning, but then made her way to the bus stop because she'd decided to take herself to her nanna's place.

'Would you like to call anyone?' a nurse asked. 'You can use the phone.'

Fred didn't want to call anyone. And for once, he was glad he didn't have his phone.

Because he knew his dad would call him.

And he wouldn't even say hello.

He'd say, 'What have you done now?'

What had he done? So many things. He'd taken alcohol on a school hike, he'd been a pain to be around, he'd run off from the group. And he'd met Tessa, carrying a bucket, one shoe on and one shoe off, in the middle of a storm.

Fred closed his eyes, remembered the stone he'd held so tightly. He reached for it again.

Tessa was safe, now.

The important thing wasn't that he'd abandoned her.

It was that he'd turned back.

•

Elle's back hurt, her ankle hurt, her knee hurt. Everything hurt! But they laughed, together.

'Chrystal, we made it.'

Diffused light hovered up ahead – the streetlights of Apollo Bay.

They collapsed on the low fencing by the side of the road. Chrystal's hair fell wet against her head, her face. Elle looked down to her muddy shoes, Chrystal with only one shoe on, their soaking, cold feet. 'We're here!' she cried with relief. 'We're out of the forest!'

'Can you hear the birds?' said Chrystal. 'Is it nearly morning?'

'Yes!' Elle hardly had the strength to stand up. 'How far do you reckon it is to Apollo Bay?' They peered towards the lights ahead. It was hard to tell. 'Three ks?' said Elle. 'Five ks? It couldn't be ten, could it? I think we've come out near Skenes Creek.'

A dairy truck roared past, lighting up the white lines on the road, the reflector posts.

'Let's try to wave down the next one,' Elle said. 'I hope they'll pick us up. I mean look at us!' They were filthy, dripping wet, injured. 'People'd think we're from some reality TV show or something. *Alone*. Or *Survivor*.'

Lights shone on the road again, coming from the opposite direction.

'It's another truck!' This one was heading out of Apollo Bay, but Elle stood and waved Chrystal's high-vis vest like a road worker, trying to get the driver's attention. It could do a U-turn, take them back.

It came closer, a ute, speeding, the lights glaring down on her. Elle jumped back as a dog barked, and the ute screamed past them, spraying mud and water over their bodies, their faces.

She turned to Chrystal. 'Was that those guys?'

They stared after the ute. 'I couldn't see,' said Chrystal.

They sat back on the low fence. Elle wiped the splattered mud from her face with the soaking sleeve of her hoodie, and then, without thinking, she reached over and wiped Chrystal's face, too, moved her wet, sand-coloured hair back behind her ear. Elle felt so tired, too tired to speak. And Chrystal was too tired to flinch or pull away, so she let Elle touch her. Chrystal didn't look at Elle directly, but past her to the ocean. The hoodie sleeve fell back and it was just Elle's fingers wiping the mud from Chrystal's face, skin on skin. And Elle wondered if everyone had this intense feeling now that people could touch each other again, or whether seeing that ute upset Chrystal, because Chrystal's eyes filled with tears.

Elle felt tears coming, too, but she managed to stop them. She had to be strong and get to Apollo Bay. It was up to her, it was always up to her. The strongest in the room. But Chrystal had been strong, too. And that was a huge relief, maybe that was why Elle's tears had started again. She pictured Chrystal, standing above them with the gun. Elle would never forget that image. She took a deep breath like Laila had taught her. Slowly and evenly. 'Please, someone, pick us up,' she said. 'We can't walk to Apollo Bay, we just can't.'

They sat. 'The sky's getting lighter,' said Elle. 'I reckon it's probably nearly six. If no one comes in ten minutes, we'll have to start walking again.'

'Listen,' said Chrystal, 'there are more birds.'

'Do you think it was them? In the ute?' If it was them, had he been in the back? Had they found him, picked him up? Elle didn't want to say his name out loud. Sean.

'I couldn't see, it was going so fast.'

'Do you think you . . . if he was hurt –'

'What did he want?' Chrystal said suddenly.

'What do you mean? He wanted to terrify us,' said Elle.

'He wanted you,' said Chrystal.

'He was cruel. Playing some kind of game.'

More birds called. Elle recognised some, but not others. 'We should start walking,' she said, but she actually couldn't get up. She was too cold, her legs were too stiff and sore. Her knee still hurt, and now her ankle was no good.

Chrystal acted as if she hadn't heard Elle at all. 'You're so pretty you could be a Victoria's Secret model. You really could.'

'Chrystal, stop saying that! As if!' Elle picked up a pebble, threw it absently. She couldn't help laughing. 'You're totally wrong! Why are you so obsessed with Victoria's Secret?'

No response.

'Anyway, Chrystal, you're pretty, too.' She was, when you really looked at her. Chrystal's face was intense, mysterious, like someone from a country Elle had never been to before. And if she washed her hair, put on some make-up . . .

'If we're so pretty,' said Chrystal, 'then why don't either of us have a boyfriend?'

'Well –'

'I know why.'

Elle smiled. Chrystal was such a one-off. 'Okay, why?'

'Mmmmmmmm we're not thin enough.'

'What?'

Chrystal twirled her hair, if she still had Snoopy she'd be pulling his ears. 'Mmmmmmmm does anyone like their body in the mirror?'

Bits of hair were entwined around her fingers.

In Elle's mind, she answered this question with a question: Was that why Chrystal never had a shower?

'Do you want a boyfriend?' Elle asked.

No answer.

'Have you ever had a boyfriend?' Elle hadn't, she had a heap of friends who were guys, but no boyfriend.

'Chrystal?'

Silence.

'Chrystal, why don't you answer people? Do you . . . get that it's rude?'

'Mmmmmmmmm there's a lot of sound, I can't hear.'

'Because of your tinnitus? But you can hear me, now. Why don't you answer me?'

A bird called.

'Mmmmmmm I don't know what people are asking.'

'My question only needs a yes or no,' said Elle. She stood up, stooped and crooked like an ancient person, looked one way then the other. Why were there no cars on this stupid road!

'Mmmmmmm only online.'

'What?' said Elle.

'Only online, is where I've had a boyfriend.'

Is *that* who she's messaging all the time? An online boyfriend?

'He turned out to be a fake.'

'Right . . .' Then, 'I'm too tall,' said Elle suddenly. 'I'm too strong.'

Chrystal laughed. 'I'm too strange.'

'You actually are quite strange. But that's okay,' Elle added quickly, 'that's fine.'

Chrystal didn't look over, but something in her face changed, and she blurted out, 'When you stay with me, you'll sleep in Daniel's room because he's away.'

Elle felt something inside her soften, felt her shoulders fall. She sat with it, this sense of letting go. And she knew then that she would go on the exchange, she would go and stay with Chrystal, meet the dad in rehab, the mum Chrystal rarely mentioned, the older brother at college. Maybe it's not a lack of feeling, Elle thought, looking at Chrystal twisting her hair, maybe Chrystal feels all the feelings, she just communicates them differently.

The world was so still, now. Magpies warbled, a kookaburra –

Chrystal pointed over Elle's shoulder, past her.

'Look. It's nearly morning.'

They watched as the first light came up over the ocean. They weren't friends, Elle knew that, not like her friends at school. Girls she shared everything with – or did she? What were they really sharing? A version of themselves that they wanted to present to the world? The person who had really seen Elle, more than anyone, was Chrystal.

The next truck stopped, the driver leant over to open the door.

'Jesus, get in, kids. What the hell happened to you?'

•

After some time, the glow worms began to fade, and Ash heard bird calls from outside the cave. 'I think it's nearly morning. We should keep going.'

They picked up their packs, as if this was their home and they were leaving it, and came out of the cave.

'It's getting light,' said Laila.

'I think so.' Ash could make out the landscape more easily.

They followed the creek, holding onto bracken and branches to steady themselves, until at last the forest began to clear a little. Laila reached for Ash's hand again.

The cold air lifted, there was a hint of warmth.

He stopped, they both stopped. Ash felt her hand on the back of his neck. Her touch went through his whole body.

They kissed again.

Salt, sweat, tang.

This magic forest, this magical girl. Would the spell be broken when they left?

She took the cave stone from her pocket, placed it in his hand. 'It's yours. To remind you.'

Ash rubbed it between his fingers. He would keep it, always.

They reached a track. Then a lookout over the water, the creek no longer black but grey now, and wider. Ash turned, felt an expanse of something.

'I can smell the ocean.'

The track led to a dirt road. 'I know where we are,' said Laila. 'I think this is the back road that comes into Apollo Bay. We must have been up on Beacon Ridge.'

As they came down to the hard gravel, Ash felt as if his feet were touching earth for the first time, as if before had been some kind of dream. A fox ran over, disappearing in a russet flash into the grasses.

A faint light appeared on the horizon.

Shimmering.

They had reached the sea.

Seventeen

The police took Fred's details, and phoned the school.

Tessa's mother was somewhere in the hospital, but she'd asked him to wait, not to leave before giving her his number. 'I want to thank you, properly,' she'd told him.

Fred dozed, sitting in the chair. He was exhausted. He kept seeing her, Tessa, in the back of the ute. When they had to push her chest down. He hoped she wouldn't have bruises. The doctor had told him that because she had a pulse they probably hadn't needed the 'chest compression', as she'd called it, only the 'assisted breathing'. 'But listen,' she'd said, 'you got her here. And in that storm, as well.'

Fred didn't want to be thanked properly. He didn't want the mother to phone him, telling him what a hero he was. When he was actually a creep. Someone who'd snuck into people's rooms at night and photographed them sleeping. Even a teacher. Ms O. In her first year of teaching. Who had been so nice to him, tried to help him. Who he really liked! And because he was stupid, stupid blind Freddy, because they'd set him up, he was the only one captured on CCTV. He could have dobbed them in, Matt and the older guys, but what was the point? He hated them, hated the place, just wanted to get away. Then his dad made Fred feel that he'd rescued him, that he owed him. People thought he was weird after that, like a stalker. But he wasn't, that wasn't him at all. Still, once everyone thought something about you, what could you do? Run away. Run away and never come back. Get your dad to save you. Again.

Fred put down the blanket, picked up his pack, walked through the big glass doors and left.

He crossed the road, headed down to the beach, which was strewn with logs, timber, an old rubbish bin, branches. Seaweed and bark were mangled together on the sand, like wild sculptures. There were even bits of roofing iron, metal pipes. As if the beach had been ransacked. But it was the only evidence of the storm the night before. Everything else was still, as if nothing had even happened.

Fred looked back to the hills behind him, the forest.

Someone from school would be coming to pick him up. He'd get in trouble again. Why had he even brought those cans with him? It wasn't as if he really wanted to get drunk. Sometimes Fred felt he wanted to ransack, too, to tear everything down, wreck everything.

But now, would he be able to start again?

He went and sat where the creek met the ocean. Ducks skimmed across the water, flying low. The sun was below the horizon, but its colour was already in the sky. Broad, wispy clouds. Light Violet, Primrose Yellow, Gold, Pink Madder Lake. The colours surrounded Fred, calming him.

Fred was someone who people had once expected a lot of, but after the failed schools, the trouble at Bellarine, the bad marks, he was becoming someone who people expected not much of. That *he* expected not much of.

But no one else was going to look after him, Fred thought, no one cared, so he had to look after his own feelings. Over the past year or so, the more alone he'd felt, the more he'd worried about his own comfort, the less he'd thought of other people. Which made people like him less, which made him feel more alone. Jesus, how had this happened to him?

And now, he might be sent home from Jess's place. Another thing that didn't work out. And where even was 'home'? Fred suddenly felt sad about that. He knew he wasn't nice to Jess. He never even asked how she was. Jess always asked how was your day, and what did you do, and Fred never answered more than a grunt. It wasn't that he couldn't be bothered telling her, he almost cried thinking about it, it was that he couldn't frame it, couldn't tell it in a way people tell a story of their day, their summer, their family, their life. And Jess's life seemed so pointless and boring. When she wasn't drawing, she was spinning wool; she had a spinning wheel and everything, got the wool sent from a farm somewhere. She'd knitted him some socks. Fred hated the greasy wool, hated the sound of Jess's foot going up and down, up and down on the treadle. The way she hunched over the contraption like an old lady. I mean how old was she? She wouldn't even be fifty yet.

Fred's parents were older, he was IVF, an only child. His mum used to say he was all she ever wanted. That was kind of ironic, now. His dad was always telling Fred about the sacrifices they'd made for him, sending him to good schools, choosing holidays that he'd enjoy. His mum never mentioned sacrifices but Fred sensed that she'd made a few. Like even to stay married for as long as she did. His parents only separated three years ago, when Fred was eleven.

Fred's dad told him that kids these days expect everything instantly. They don't know how lucky they are. Like life is so easy for them. What, Fred felt like yelling at him, like destruction of the world, like climate change, like parents who can't fit their son into their lives anymore. Like global pandemics, and losing those years. Like people being cancelled all the time. Like the end of forgiveness. And trust. Like it's not easy. His dad was a psychiatrist and everything, but Fred knew that was no protection at all.

Did his dad even know he was here, that he had gone on the dropping? Would Jess have let his mother know? He imagined his dad getting a call, another call about his stupid son.

And the whole thing really had been his fault. Because he had the booze, he'd put the torches and stuff in with it. And then one thing had led to another. Still, if he hadn't run off up that hill, would anyone else have found Tessa? Would she have survived that storm out there on her own?

Fred looked at the colours of the creek. Sap Green, Cedar Green, Bronze. Sepia. The creek was higher than usual, and bits of vine had caught and hung like ruined bunting from the fallen branches. He noticed a tall stalk, a curled, purple flower, and then . . .

236

What was that? Something black and white, wedged between rocks at the edge.

Fred scrambled down to it.

•

As they came into Apollo Bay, Elle saw the shops, none open yet. In the window of the hardware store sat a stack of red buckets. They looked so innocent, like something from a picture book.

Elle used the truck driver's mobile to call the school. Sammi was coming to Apollo Bay in the van to collect them. They'd probably have to take Chrystal straight to the hospital. It was nearly six-thirty now. Elle was so grateful that it was getting light, and that awful, endless night was finally over. The truck driver dropped them at the service station.

'I wish we had some money,' said Elle, 'we could get something to eat.' They headed over the road and down the sandy path to the beach, Chrystal hopping and leaning on Elle's shoulder. She-oaks waved gently in the breeze. The dawn light shone pink through the grasses by the sand, with their pale grey and green stalks. From a distance they looked soft, but they were sharp.

Elle looked along the beach towards the breakwater.

It was morning, but the time felt unreal, not like the previous morning when they'd woken up, eaten pancakes in the kitchen and talked about the weather. It seemed vague, like there was no rhythm to the hours anymore. Elle felt this whenever she'd stayed up all night on a sleepover, or on a long flight from one side of the world to the other. The time in the forest was like she'd been underwater, or dreaming, her senses working differently, and only just now she'd woken up.

Two figures on the stone wall.

Elle looked closer.

Was that Ash and Laila?

'Stay here,' said Elle, and she was sprinting, her exhaustion, her sore ankle forgotten, calling, running across the hard, low-tide sand.

•

Fred put his stuff down and stood at the water's edge. The whole sky was pink. Pink Madder Lake. Jess had bought some pencils for him because she'd seen him looking at hers, she thought he might like to draw. He hadn't even said thank you. Hadn't even opened them. Didn't even know where he'd put them. Had forgotten about it until now. The seventy-two pack costs over a hundred dollars, and he knew Jess had hardly any money. His mum paid her to have him there. Maybe his mum paid her for the Derwents, but Fred had the feeling this was something that Jess might have done on her own. Now he felt terrible that he hadn't said thank you. Hadn't even listened when she told him what a lake pigment was. Fred knew that something in him still wanted those pencils. To draw on the thick, creamy paper. But he'd forgotten how, he didn't know how to do that anymore. Fred turned around, slowly spinning, his eyes adjusting and seeing all the colours, as if the dots in a Seurat painting were becoming one. A whole picture. The forest behind him, the silver sea, the sky.

The sea was calm. Fred breathed in, held his arms out. He hoped no one saw. Jesus, he was turning into Laila! Next he'd start that annoying chanting. He took the black stone from his pocket, the stone he stole, raised his hand to throw it in . . .

Something made him turn. Up by the breakwater he saw figures sitting on the sand.

Fred picked up his pack and started walking.

As he got closer, he realised it was the others.

Elle, Chrystal, Ash and Laila.

He waved. Would they want to see him?

He'd almost reached them when Ash called out.

'Hey, Fred!'

They did seem genuinely pleased. That he was okay, anyway.

'Hi.' He stood, they sat. Elle had taken off her shoes and socks. Her feet were wrinkly and red, like when you've been in the surf for hours.

'Where did you get to?' Ash asked, after a moment.

Fred threw himself down on the sand. 'You don't want to know. It's a long story.'

Would he ever tell it? Every detail? Did that even matter? 'But that little kid on the bus, Ash, she was in the forest. I . . . I ran into her.'

'What! Really?'

'Yeah, like I said it's a long story, but she's at the hospital now.'

'The hospital?' said Elle. 'Is she okay?'

'Tessa, her name was I think?' said Ash.

'Yeah, Tessa,' said Fred. 'Yeah, she's okay.' He breathed out, a long, heavy sigh. 'What happened to you guys?'

'Same. Long story.' Ash lay back, sprawled on the sand.

'At least we're all okay. And we got out of that bloody forest.'

The others smiled, which made Fred feel better. He noticed that Chrystal's shoes and socks were off as well. Her right ankle was a purple lump, swollen up like a pomegranate.

'What happened to you?'

No answer.

'She twisted it,' said Elle.

'Looks painful,' said Fred. He turned to Ash. 'What did you do to your face?'

Ash had forgotten, he put his hand to his cheek, felt the ragged graze. 'It got scratched. It doesn't hurt.'

'Where did you find that little girl?' Elle asked him. 'How did you get back here?'

There would be time to tell them about what happened. For all of them to tell their stories.

Fred didn't answer Elle. Instead, he reached into his backpack.

'Hey, Chrystal.'

No response.

'Look what else I found.'

He held out wet, bedraggled Snoopy. Fred had squeezed most of the water out of it, so Snoopy's shape was odd, and he had a kind of bemused look on his face, a twisted smile.

Chrystal let out a tiny gasp, and seemed for a second to look at Snoopy as if she didn't recognise him. But she took him all the same. 'Thank you,' she said, and Fred felt good. Chrystal put Snoopy straight in her pack.

He turned to Laila, who was sitting cross-legged on the sand. 'I've got something for you as well.'

He held out his hand, and the black tourmaline. 'I took that stone.'

Would she be angry with him?

'If you took it, you must have needed it,' said Laila.

'Yeah, I think I probably did.' Fred sighed, laughed.

Yeah Fred, not so cynical now, thought Elle, but she stayed quiet.

'I'm giving it back,' said Fred, his arm outstretched.

'No, it's yours,' said Laila. 'To keep.'

'Oh, okay, ah . . . thanks.' Fred was a cynical person, but even he believed that maybe that stone had helped a bit.

'We're all here!' said Ash suddenly. 'We survived!' He punched Elle playfully on the shoulder. 'Well done, leader.'

'I didn't exactly do a great job,' said Elle. 'I couldn't keep us together. I made some dumb decisions. We all split up . . . then Chrystal had to save me,' she added. And something dawned on Elle, something no one had ever told her in the leadership courses – that resilience can be a double-edged sword.

'You might have done a better job,' she told Ash.

'I don't think so. But yeah, I was a bit pissed when you were made leader and not me.'

There. He'd said it. 'Laila rescued me, too, by the way. I fell in the creek.'

'Elle also rescued me,' said Chrystal, and everyone turned to her, because they weren't used to Chrystal participating in a regular conversation.

'And Chrystal rescued me!' said Elle.

'Really?' said Laila, surprised.

'She did.' Elle smiled at Chrystal. How brave, how strong she had been. 'Actually, Chrystal rescued all of us, when lightning struck that tree.'

'What tree?' said Fred.

'This huge tree,' said Ash, 'it literally caught on fire. Did you see all that lightning?'

Fred nodded.

It was funny, Elle would never have imagined that anyone would rescue her – not Fred, not Ash, not even Laila, and certainly not Chrystal.

'Looks like I'm the only one who didn't rescue anyone.' Ash smiled. But the way Laila looked at him made him wonder whether he'd maybe rescued her in some way, too.

'And Chrystal fired a gun!'

'Shit, what?' said Fred. 'You what?'

'Yeah,' said Elle, 'that guy Sean came back . . .'

'Who's Sean?' Fred asked, and Chrystal hummed, and even Elle felt a deep shaking start up through her body. She wasn't ready to talk about that. Neither of them were. Quickly she changed the subject, turned to Ash and Laila. 'What about you guys?'

'Yeah,' said Fred, 'did you split up too? What happened to you?'

Ash and Laila looked knowingly at each other, as if they had a secret.

For a moment, Ash was lost for words. How could he explain what happened in the cave? Did he even want to? Ash had seen a lot of people who relied on instinct, deep knowledge, and connection to the land and the rocks and the water, and it gave them everything. Life. Meaning. Where earth and time exist as one. Something mysterious had happened to them in the cave. He didn't know what it was, but he trusted it.

'We got lost,' he said eventually, 'we followed an owl, we found the creek. I fell in, and like I said,' Ash laughed, 'Laila rescued me.'

'You would have got out,' said Laila. 'I just gave you a hand.' Then, 'Hey,' she said, and pointed at the perfect, round moon, translucent now, still visible on one side of the sky, with the sun rising on the other. 'Maybe the moon was guiding us all along.'

Ash looked out towards the sea. An even, dusky blue, almost transparent, was fading to pink on the horizon. They should feel tired, they had been up all night. But Ash felt invigorated, like they'd all just woken from a long sleep. 'See that blue,' he said, 'I think that's my favourite colour.'

'At last!' said Fred. 'One favourite thing! Next, the death-row meal. Which reminds me, I'm actually starving. I'd kill for some hot chips.'

'Me too,' said Elle.

The others all agreed. Fred watched the dawn light their faces. Rose Pink. He felt himself wanting to speak again, and for once he said what he really wanted to say.

'I'm sorry, that I ran off when I did. I'm sorry about the drinks, sorry I was such a dickhead, and . . .' He ran out of words because suddenly he felt so light. He hadn't given part of himself up, or away. He felt strangely free, as if he could get up and run along this long flat beach in the sunrise forever.

Ash used to think that there were good people and bad people and once you knew who was who, it was easy to work out and things would be consistent. But looking at Fred, he realised that it's so much more complicated than that. He was about to say 'Sure, that's okay,' when Fred burst out, 'Hey, isn't this morning beautiful?'

It was a very un-Fred thing to say. And it was like they didn't need to talk about the night anymore, just then. It would be a while before they talked about it much at all.

Fred was right, the morning was beautiful. A strip of orange-pink lit up the horizon, separating sky from sea. Was there a name for that colour? Maybe Fred would invent one. Now golden light streamed through gaps in the morning cloud – light grey, dark grey, almost purple. Sunrise changed so quickly. If you walked away for five minutes, or looked at your phone, it could be gone, replaced by regular daylight. As if that moment of magic hadn't happened, wouldn't happen in another unique way tomorrow, the next day, forever. Fleeting. Maybe Fred could see why people came from all over the world to be here. The Great Ocean Road. Such a majestic name. Now pink stratas lined the grey. The route to school, yes, but such a majestic name.

'You'll need to get your ankle X-rayed,' said Ash. 'Look how swollen it is.'

'Does it hurt much?' Laila asked.

'Chrystal?' Elle prompted her.

'Not much,' said Chrystal, looking out towards the sea.

'Lol we went on a dropping and came back with an *extra* person. Tessa. I bet that's never happened before.' Fred's eyes crinkled up, and Elle realised that she'd never seen him smile naturally. He looked so different, his whole body, like something inside him had finally surrendered.

Ash was playing with a ball of damp sand, tossing it in his hands.

Elle rubbed her ankle. She'd need time for everything that had happened to settle in her head. And to think Chrystal had only been worried about a storm . . .

The sun sent its first soft rays over the water. They could feel it already, warming them, drying them out. A gentle breeze made ripples in the shallows. Nothing was wild, everything was beginning again.

'We better go up to the main street,' said Elle. 'Sammi should be here soon.'

They stood up, and Elle reached out, felt the energy that Laila always talked about as they linked arms, all five of them, and went up the beach, over the sandy grasses, and out into the day.

ACKNOWLEDGEMENTS

Heartfelt thanks to Jeanmarie Morosin, Karen Ward and everyone at Hachette for always being so warm, encouraging and professional. And to Deonie Fiford for another thoughtful and wise copyedit.

Thanks to my agent, Pippa Masson at Curtis Brown, for her ongoing support.

Thanks to David Dean who created a wonderfully dramatic and arresting cover.

Thanks also to the various family members who accompanied me on night walks into the forest when I felt too uneasy to venture in alone – Cait, Lulu, Mum, Lizzie and Michael.

Huge thanks to Davina Bell and Michael Wagner for reading early drafts and providing insightful and valuable feedback.

I'm grateful to my extended family for their love and support, and thanks always to Michael, Wil, Lizzie and Mitch.

Jane Godwin is the highly acclaimed and internationally published author of many books for children and young people, across all styles and ages. Children's Publisher at Penguin Books Australia for many years, Jane was the co-creator with Davina Bell of the Our Australian Girl series of quality historical fiction for middle readers. Jane's books include her novels *Falling from Grace*, *As Happy as Here* (a CBCA Notable Book) and *When Rain Turns to Snow* (shortlisted for the CBCA Book of the Year for Older Readers and for the Prime Minister's Literary Awards) and picture books *Go Go and the Silver Shoes* (illustrated by Anna Walker), *The Silver Sea* (with Alison Lester and patients at the Royal Children's Hospital, Melbourne) and *Watch This!* (with designer Beci Orpin and photographer Hilary Walker). Jane is dedicated to pursuing quality and enriching reading and writing experiences for young people, and spends as much time as she can working with them in schools and communities and running literature and writing programs.

janegodwin.com.au